THE OTHER SIDE OF TRUTH

BEVERLEY NAIDOO

⊞HARPERTROPHY®
AN IMPRINT OF HARPERCOLLINS*PUBLISHERS*

Amistad

Amistad is an imprint of HarperCollins Publishers.

Harper Trophy® is a registered trademark of
HarperCollins Publishers Inc.

The Other Side of Truth

Library of Congress Cataloging-in-Publication Data
Naidoo, Beverley.
The other side of truth / by Beverley Naidoo.
p.   cm.
Summary: Smuggled out of Nigeria after their mother's murder,
Sade and her younger brother are abandoned in London when
their uncle fails to meet them at the airport and they are fearful of
their new surroundings and of what may have happened to their
journalist father back in Nigeria.
ISBN 0-06-029628-3 — ISBN 0-06-029629-1 (lib. bdg.)
ISBN 0-06-441002-1 (pbk.)
1. Nigerians—England—London—Juvenile fiction. [1.
Nigerians—England—London—Fiction.   2. Refugees—Fiction.
3. Brothers and sisters—Fiction.]   I. Title.
PZ7.N1384 Ot 2001   00-054112
[Fic]—dc21   CIP
                                                AC

Typography by Hilary Zarycky
❖
First Harper Trophy edition, 2003
Originally published in 2000 by Puffin Books, a division of the
Penguin Group, London, England.

Visit us on the World Wide Web!
www.harperchildrens.com

On a huge hill,
Cragged, and steep, Truth stands, and he that will
Reach her, about must, and about must go . . .
JOHN DONNE

To all young people
who wish to know more

FOREWORD

Beverley Naidoo has struck home again, bringing together the critical themes of political oppression, exile, Africa, and childhood. *The Other Side of Truth* has resonances of the execution of the Nigerian writer Ken Saro-Wiwa. But this is no dry polemic about freedom of speech—it's a fast and vivid account of a family's flight from threat and murder seen through the eyes of twelve-year-old Sade and her ten-year-old brother, Femi. Deservedly the winner of a UK Arts Council Award for work in progress, this is a wonderfully accessible story laced with powerful messages of family commitment and human rights. Beverley Naidoo's own South African origins and subsequent exile in London provide heartfelt spine to this book. For this is a novel that flows from the same source as the award-winning *Journey to Jo'burg*—banned in South Africa until 1991. Not only a marvelous read but one that refuels the desire for justice and freedom within and beyond our shores.

JON SNOW
July 1999

GUIDE TO PRONUNCIATION

Sade (short for *Folasade*) is a name in Yoruba, a language with a very musical sound. *Sade* is pronounced something like *Shad-deh*, with your voice rising on the second syllable.

ACKNOWLEDGMENTS

I owe thanks to many people who have generously given their time and knowledge during the research and writing of this novel. I, of course, take full responsibility for the fiction.

For the knowledge I have gained of Nigeria over the years, I thank two families in particular. The Oke family—with special thanks to Dr. Adetinuke Tadese for her comments on my manuscript and to her parents for a lifetime friendship and the integrity of their vision. Also the Oyeleye family for a wealth of insight—with special thanks to Olusola Oyeleye, not only for her encouragement and comments but for introducing me to her mother's proverbs before introducing me to her mother.

There are many other individuals, establishments, and organizations concerned with refugee children and asylum seekers whom I wish to thank. Unfortunately, they are too many to name in all but I would like to offer special thanks to: Jennifer Abuah of the Refugee Advisory Project; child psychotherapist Sheila Melzak of the Medical Foundation for the Care of Victims of Torture; David Verity-Smith; Jill Rutter and Terry Smith of the Refugee Council; Sheila Kasabova of Camden Refugee Education Project; Jeanette Redding of Enfield Refugee Education Team; Enfield Language and Curriculum Access Service staff and their students at Kingsmead and Lea Valley High School; Annie Donaldson and her students at Warwick Park School in Southwark.

I thank all those who read and commented on my manuscript with a special thank-you to Zora Laattoe. Thanks, as ever, to my family for their various supportive roles. Finally, thank you to the Arts Council of England for support and acknowledgment in the form of a generous Writers' Award.

THE OTHER SIDE OF TRUTH

CHAPTER 1

SURVIVORS

SADE IS SLIPPING HER ENGLISH BOOK into her schoolbag when *Mama screams. Two sharp cracks splinter the air. She hears her father's fierce cry, rising, falling.*

"No! No!"

The revving of a car and skidding of tires smother his voice.

Her bag topples from the bed, spilling books, pen and pencil onto the floor. She races to the verandah, pushing past Femi in the doorway. His body is wooden with fright.

"Mama mi?" she whispers.

Papa is kneeling in the driveway, Mama partly curled up against him. One bare leg stretches out in front of her. His strong hands grip her, trying to halt the growing scarlet monster. But it has already spread down her bright white nurse's uniform. It stains the earth around them.

A few seconds, that is all. Later, it will always seem much longer.

A small gathering began to swell the house, tense and hushed. Sade stared numbly out of the sitting-room window to where

3

Joseph stood nervously on guard. At each new bang, rattle or hoot, he peered anxiously through the crack between the metal gates. His head moved painfully forward and backward like that of an old tortoise. His fingers floundered and fumbled each time he had to wrench back the bolt. He had been a witness. One second he had been casually pushing back one of the gates so his master could drive off to work. The next second, his madame lay slumped on the ground and a white car was screeching away through the wide avenue of palm trees.

Uncle Tunde, Papa's eldest brother, arrived with the doctor. Sade and Femi huddled close to their father as he steered the doctor to the sofa where Mama now lay. Her face stared upward to the ceiling fan, with lips slightly parted and a tiny frown, as if there were only some small disturbance in a dream. But the flowers on the embroidered bedspread wrapped around her were drenched in crimson and told a different story. Sade clutched her brother's hand, waiting.

"I am very sorry, Mr. Solaja. Your wife had no chance. Straight into the heart." The doctor pronounced the verdict in a low purr. "I shall inform the authorities—and, if you wish, New Era Hospital? For the post-mortem."

Papa, usually brimming over with words, simply nodded. His arms drew the children in tightly as a high trembling voice quivered next to them. Mama Buki's cry wailed like a lonely seabird.

"Sista mi! Sista mi!"

Sade's own voice was lost somewhere deep inside her. She wanted to rush across, grab hold of Mama, squeeze breath back into her—before it was too late—but she could not move. Kneeling beside her sister, Mama Buki's tears swept over her broad cheeks as she covered Mama's face with the corner of the embroidered bedspread. Sade watched in horror, her own silent tears trapped within her, like in a stone.

Grief burst around them like a pierced boil. All about her, Sade heard people repeat fragments of the story. Mr. Falana, one of their neighbors and also Papa's editor-in-chief, had heard both the gunshots and the getaway car. In the deathly hush that followed, he had peeped out from his own gate on the other side of the road. Seeing the entrance to the Solaja house wide open, he feared the worst and rushed across, followed by his wife still in her dressing gown. It was he who had helped Papa carry Mama inside. Now he had to hurry away to warn his other staff. Papa was the most outspoken journalist on *Speak*, one of the weekly newspapers in English, but he might not be the only target. Even before any newspaper headlines, the news would be darting by word and mouth along the pavements, highways and cables of Lagos. When the news reached Mama's friends at the hospital where she worked, there would be no end of visitors. Suffocated by arms and voices and with the echo of the gunshots still in her head, Sade felt the urge to escape.

"Please . . ."

The effort was great and her voice was small. But it worked and Sade maneuvered her way out. Papa's study would be quiet.

As she entered the study, the telephone rang. Automatically she picked it up, covering one ear to hear more easily.

"Is that the home of Mr. Folarin Solaja who writes for *Speak*?"

The man's voice was soft but perfectly clear.

"Yes."

"Don't trouble him. Just give him a message. Tell him: if we get the family first, what does it matter?"

The voice wrung the breath out of her, like a snake secretly squeezing her throat. Frantically she signaled to Uncle Tunde who had come to the study door. He strode across to Papa's desk, but as he reached for the receiver, there was a click. Sade struggled to repeat the horrible words. Her uncle's thick graying eyebrows lurched up over his gold-rimmed spectacles. He looked very grave.

A little later, Joseph unlocked the gates for a sleek white ambulance. The small crowd of mourners stood aside to make a pathway for the two men with a stretcher. Mama Buki led the hymn singing. Barely two minutes later, pressed between Mama Buki's heaving, swaying body and her father who was silent and almost perfectly still, Sade watched them carry Mama away under a blinding-white sheet. The ambulance door clicked shut. The windows were darkened glass and Sade could no longer even see the sheet. Everyone fell quiet. The only sound was of the ambulance's motor and of Joseph grappling once again with the gates. His old body pulled to attention as the vehicle backed out, as if in a final salute. That was all. Mama was gone.

Uncle Tunde led Papa gently away. The plum-colored swirls on Papa's tunic were splattered with gashes of a deeper scarlet—their mother's blood.

"Take care of the children, please," Papa murmured to Mama Buki. "I need to—"

He gestured with both hands toward his clothes. Mama Buki, her eyes red and watery, shepherded Sade and Femi toward the kitchen. But as she turned to share her grief with a friend, Sade and Femi exchanged glances and wove their way back through the cluster of mourners. Sade caught snatches of phrases, Yoruba mingled with English.

"*O ma se o!* What a pity!"

". . . such a good good woman"

". . . evil people"

". . . he was their target"

". . . bread of sorrow"

". . . saved him"

Sade studied her own clothes. Not a speck, not a stain on her gray school skirt and blue blouse to show what terrible thing had happened. She ran to her room, feeling impelled to strip away the uniform. If only by putting on something fresh and new, they could begin the day again. She brushed her fingers along a line of clothes. Colors of sea, forests, flowers and birds. Her fingers, however, came to rest on a soft, black velvet dress with a white lace collar that Mama had made for her when Papa's father died. She wanted to lie down and make everything stop. But Femi was outside, calling her name, his voice urgent.

"Come," he insisted, when she opened the door.

Grabbing her hand, he led her to Papa's study, ignoring the room with visitors.

7

Sade fully expected Uncle Tunde would tell them to leave when they crept into the study. He was leaning against Papa's desk, in his sober black suit, the one he wore on days he was meant to be in court. Papa often used to tease him. "Be free like me! I wear what I like to work!" Uncle Tunde paused to acknowledge the children. His gray-flecked beard made his face look square and solid. It was a family joke that his hair was becoming the color of a judge's wig. Papa, seated beside the desk in a full-length ink-black *agbada*, hardly seemed to notice as they settled themselves by the untidy side table stacked with books and papers.

It was usually their father whose arms, hands, even fingers, danced liked furious gymnasts whenever he argued or talked about things that fired him up. It was usually their uncle who folded his arms as he listened. If you are a lawyer, Uncle Tunde had told Sade, you need to keep cool and listen very carefully. But today their father's arms hung without life. It was his older brother whose hands pleaded along with his voice.

"They're not finished with you, Folarin! They won't stop until they've shut you up. You know what that means! You've gone too far with them now."

Their father always took chances with what he wrote. He said nothing now, but Sade knew his words.

The truth is the truth. How can I write what's untrue?

Sade knew how worried Mama had been about his latest article. But Sade had never heard Mama try to stop him, like Uncle Tunde did.

Their uncle stretched across the desk to pick up a newspaper. One hand resting on their father's shoulder, he began to read aloud: "Why do the Brass Buttons who rule over us spend millions of naira sending their children to the most expensive schools and colleges in England and America? How does a soldier—even a general—acquire so much money? And what about our own schools and colleges here in Nigeria? Our Brass Button generals shut them down when teachers complain they have not been paid and when students complain they have no books. It seems they can still sleep easily in their beds even though hundreds of thousands of our own children are not being taught. What a disgrace for a country that held some of the finest universities and schools in Africa! But then our Commander-in-Chief believes more in buttons than brains."

Normally Papa would have flared up.

Every word of that is true.

But today he was mute. His face was turned to the window that overlooked the front gate where the car had stopped. Their uncle slid the newspaper back on to the desk.

"You call your article 'Our Children's Future.' What do you imagine will happen now to your own, Folarin?"

Uncle Tunde stared across at the two children. Femi chewed on his thumb. Sade sensed the tightness of his body, small for a ten-year-old but tough as wire, Mama used to say. Sade felt riveted to her chair. In all her twelve years she had never heard her uncle, or any grown-up, talk quite like this. Normally she and Femi would have been sent outside or to another room. Nor had she ever seen Papa like this before, as if his spirit had flown out from him. Uncle Tunde still did not hold back.

"Look, Folarin, we all know how brave you are. Braver than most of us. But are you wise? You say our country must have writers to tell the truth. But, tell me, what can you write from the grave?"

Scent from the pink magnolia beyond the window bars drifted inside and Papa continued to gaze quietly at the window.

"For goodness sake, Folarin, look at what they've just done to Ken! The whole world was shouting 'Saro-Wiwa must not hang!' But did His Excellency Commander-in-Chief, General Abacha, and his soldiers care? Of course not! So what will hold them back with an unknown writer called Solaja? To them you are just another troublemaking pen-pusher. Look, if you get out of here—join Dele in London—at least you can go on writing. Let the outside world know what's happening to Nigeria. What good is the truth on the lips of a dead journalist? And in that state, you wouldn't be much good to your children either."

Femi couldn't take any more. Pushing back his chair, he ran to their father. Sade followed, as if to protect him from further attack. From the government's secret bullets or from Uncle Tunde's razor-sharp words? She was not quite sure.

Papa's arms, a moment ago so listless, enclosed them both firmly. Nestling in the folds of his tunic, Sade curled her fingers through Papa's and was relieved to feel him responding. Uncle Tunde stood watching. He had said enough.

"Your uncle is right," their father said finally. "We need to get away for a while."

"Grandma will hide us! We can go to Family House!" Femi cried.

Papa shook his head.

"Even Family House won't be safe. These people mean business. They know our village and I don't want them coming near Grandma." Grandma was Mama's mother. Papa paused after her name.

"I should have listened to your mother."

So Mama had tried to warn Papa after all. Privately, out of the children's hearing. Yes, that would have been her way. And suddenly great awful sobs rose up inside Sade, shaking her, making her tremble. She heard her own strange sounds as she desperately sucked in gasps of air, feeling Femi stiff and silent beside her. Uncle Tunde slipped from the room, closing the door behind him on three figures clasped together like survivors on a tiny raft.

CHAPTER 2

"SAY NOTHING!"

"SAY NOTHING!" SAID UNCLE TUNDE. "It's safer for everyone that way."

They needed passports—quickly—and Uncle Tunde was setting out that very day to find how they could get them. In secret. Sade and Femi did not have passports and the police had seized Papa's only a month ago. Just a few hours before Papa had been due to leave for the airport, six strapping policemen had stormed into their house. They had pushed their way into their parents' bedroom. Sade had been helping Papa pack his bag. He had been telling her about the conference. People from many different countries were going to discuss human rights and whether their governments treated people fairly. The uninvited policemen had surrounded them like a swarm of giant locusts. One had tipped all the contents of the carefully packed suitcase onto the bed, including the shirts Sade had helped to fold. Another had snatched papers from a bedside table. Another had demanded her father's passport.

Uncle Tunde insisted on going by himself. Under no circumstances was Papa to leave the house. Papa and the children were also to keep away from the front yard. It was unlikely the gunmen would return with so many people around, but who could be sure? Everything was so unreal, including Uncle Tunde—always the cautious lawyer—setting out on a mission to acquire false passports that could take them out of the country.

"But I have to tell Kole. He's my best friend," Femi complained to Sade after Uncle Tunde had driven off. They were alone in the back compound, standing between the lofty pawpaw trees that Femi used for one of his goals. At the far end of the yard, two flaming forest trees formed the opposite goal under an umbrella of fiery red flowers. Kicking a pebble toward a clump of lemon grass, Femi raised a small spray of dust.

'You can't! Don't you understand what Uncle Tunde said?"

"But Kole can keep a secret!"

"Look, even Mama Buki doesn't know yet. If Uncle Tunde gets caught he's in big trouble. You heard him."

"I don't want to go to London," Femi whined.

Sade sighed. She was trying hard not to let herself think too much. After those great sobs had subsided earlier, her mind had become almost numb. Everything was happening too quickly. She did not want to hear Femi's complaints because she did not dare let herself think about everyone and everything she would have to leave. It was too much. She ached to hear Mama's voice calling them, to see Mama appear at the back door with her warm smile and welcoming eyes. Mama who would reassure them when they were sad or frightened. Mama who would remain calm and upright even

13

that time when the police took Papa away.

"Come to the kitchen," Sade said abruptly although she did not feel like eating. "I'm sure Mama Buki is making something."

Femi scowled and shrugged his shoulders.

"Leave me alone."

When Uncle Tunde returned some hours later in the afternoon, he headed straight for the study with their father. A few minutes later, he invited in the children.

"I've told your father that it's going to take a little time to get him a good passport. It will also be safer if he travels on his own." Uncle Tunde gazed down at his gold-rimmed spectacles dangling from his right thumb and finger. He seemed to be thinking about how to continue.

"However, by God's grace, there is a lady going to London who is prepared to take you as her children."

Sade and Femi stared, not understanding.

"Her name is Mrs. Bankole. She has a British passport with a girl and boy on it—just the right ages for you both—but they aren't traveling with her. She has agreed to say you are her children—and also to take you to your Uncle Dele."

Uncle Tunde was expecting them to go along with a lie! Both children turned anxiously to Papa.

"But she's not our mother!" Femi's face was contorted.

Their father closed his eyes. When they opened, they wavered unsteadily, as if hurt by the light.

"Of course I want us to travel together," he began. "But these people your uncle met know much more than I do about this"—he hesitated, looking from Femi to Sade—"this business of getting out of the country. And the main thing— the most important thing—is that we all end up safely together in London. We can't afford to miss this chance to get you out safely."

"We don't have much choice—and we certainly don't have much time." Uncle Tunde no longer hid his agitation. "I was told it is usually very hard to get the right passport for a child—and here we have the chance to get the two of you out together! You must realize that we are only doing this because those people who killed your dear mama will stop at nothing!"

Sade bit her lip. She and Femi were already swinging as loosely as Uncle Tunde's glasses.

"So when do we have to go?"

Uncle Tunde and Papa glanced at each other to see who would answer.

"Tonight," their father said very quietly.

CHAPTER 3

A SMALL BAG AND A RUCKSACK EACH

A SMALL BAG AND A RUCKSACK EACH. And less than an hour to pack. Only Mama Buki was told. Uncle Tunde took her outside, to the back of the house, away from the women in the kitchen. His strong whisper, however, carried through the open window of Sade's bedroom. Sade tiptoed a little nearer to the net curtain.

"If they know Folarin's children are in London, they will keep special watch at the airport. Until he is well away, let everyone think the children are in the country with relatives."

Sade knew who her uncle meant by "they"—people who hated her father because he wrote the truth.

A sudden slamming of the bedroom door behind her startled Sade and also brought the conversation outside to an abrupt stop. Femi, his back to the door, stood poised like a boxer set to fight but who cannot find his opponent. His eyes were full of misery.

"What should we take?" asked Sade.

When Femi did not reply, she opened her cupboard and stared at its contents.

Mama Buki entered the bedroom. Silently she wrapped

her arms around Sade. Femi edged away, but Mama Buki reached out and pulled him in. Slowly Sade felt him soften a little as their aunt pressed them close and murmured a short prayer for God to keep them safe. Her body was warm and sticky with the heat of the day. If only they could fall asleep and wake up to find everything had been a bad dream! But there was no way of blotting out the sounds of weeping, prayers and shocked voices that continued to thread through the house, even underneath the closed door.

When Mama Buki released the children, she worked quickly.

"It will be cold in London. Your Uncle Dele will have to get you some warm clothes right away," she said.

Neither Sade nor Femi said anything.

"Is this light sweater all you have, Sade?"

Sade nodded.

"Fit it in your rucksack. You'll need it on the plane. We shall have to find a sweatshirt for Femi."

Mama Buki now spoke as if they were making a quite ordinary journey. Sade tried to think what special things she should take with her. It was impossible to grasp that she would not be seeing her home again for what might be a long—a very long—time. Whatever she took had to be small. What would happen to her desk? After her last school report, Papa had asked a carpenter to make it for her specially. The wood even came from the forest behind Family House in their village near Ibadan. Both Mama and Papa had been born there into neighboring families although only Mama's mother was still alive. Grandma presided over the same

17

house where Mama had been a girl and Papa the boy next door. Sade loved the desk's gleaming dark wood and the curves within the perfectly planed surfaces. They reminded her of the winding paths that led deep into the forest. All that was to be left behind. Could she at least take her favorite ornament—the head of a young woman with beautifully patterned hair? Her very own young Iyawo who seemed to hold some special secret as she watched Sade do her homework. Sade picked up the ebony head. She needed both hands. It was far too heavy. She put her down, next to her partner. The head of a young man, Oko, with heavy-lidded, rather sorrowful eyes above fine narrow cheeks. Let them at least stay together. On her desk.

"What about this, Sade?"

Mama Buki held up the *aso-oke* that Sade had worn to the last family wedding. Mama had made splendid new clothes for all four of them from the same deep-blue material woven with golden thread. Sade felt her eyes pricking again.

"I don't know, Auntie," she said quickly.

"Let me roll them up small anyway. You need one good outfit, wherever you are."

How could she ever wear it again? thought Sade. The last time they had all been so happy. Mama had sat up late every night for a month sewing the wedding clothes. Sade remembered saying that the blue shone like the sea at Leki Beach at sunrise and Femi had joked that Mama was sewing up the sea. At least the outfit would help her keep that memory. From the bottom drawer of the chest, she lifted out a small bag in the same material. Mama had made it specially for her, lining the inside with shimmering blue satin. Blinking back new tears, Sade slipped it down the side of the holdall.

Mama Buki packed for Femi, asking Sade to fetch what she needed. Femi sat listlessly on the chair by Sade's desk. When Sade asked if he wanted to take his cards and his game of Ayo, he shrugged his shoulders. She put the pebbles and the board into his rucksack all the same.

Their father came to say good-bye. He sat uneasily on the edge of the bed.

"Don't worry, I shall be with you soon. Your Uncle Dele is going to take good care of you. We shall speak to him tonight when he gets back from work."

Uncle Tunde had already tried to get Uncle Dele at his flat in London, but no one had answered the telephone.

"If he can't get to the airport, Mrs. Bankole will take you to the college where he teaches." Papa handed Sade a piece of paper with his neat handwriting. At the top was written LONDON COLLEGE OF ART with an address.

"When you get there, ask for Doctor Solaja. But before that, take care. Until you are safely there, your surname is Bankole and you must only use the names in the passport." He paused grimly.

"You know how much I hate lying, but right now we have no choice."

The children listened to their father in silence. Outside, the compound lay drowsy in the still, dry heat of the sun. It was harmattan season, when winds from the Sahara blew south, shrouding everything in fine misty dust. This was the time in the afternoon when Sade liked to seek refuge in her father's study. The large revolving fan made waves of cool air dance throughout the room. Often Papa was away at the office, but even when he was at home he would let her clear aside the books on the small side table. Although he would be absorbed in his writing, she loved it when he was there. Mama would bring them each a drink at five o'clock, sometimes joking about "beans from the same pod." Then, as the sun began to go down, Femi would pester Papa to play football with him between the pawpaw and flaming forest trees.

Papa was waiting for them to respond. Femi flinched as Mama Buki placed her hands on his shoulders.

"Your father is doing what is best for you. We shall all miss you." Their aunt struggled to keep her words steady.

Sade's voice was choked. How could she speak without becoming confused and jumbled? Yet if she did not use these few minutes, when would they see Papa again and be able to talk to him face to face? She sat down beside him, leaning her head against his chest. Femi inched toward him and Papa drew him closer. Feeling the strength of Papa's arm around her, Sade heard herself ask in a small voice, "What will they do to Mama?"

She was taken aback at her own question. She did not want to think of Mama laid out on the stretcher. Yet she needed to know.

"The doctors have to do a post-mortem. They must check what is the cause of death. When that is over, she can be prepared for burial." Papa spoke gently.

"Where?" Femi asked gruffly, his head down.

"In our home village, if possible. We have to see. Look,

we shall still be able to talk over the phone and—"

Papa broke off as Uncle Tunde poked his head around the door.

"Sorry to interrupt. It's time to leave. We have to get through the traffic."

Uncle Tunde had driven his car around to the back compound.

"It's better if no one sees you," he said bluntly.

He opened the rear door and pointed to the floor between the seats.

"Squeeze in down here and I shall cover you up."

A dark gray blanket lay on the backseat.

Femi's face wrinkled in protest.

"You can be sure your uncle will make me lie down there when we go out!" Papa embraced the children quickly.

"Look after each other," he said huskily. "We shall be together soon. *O dabo.*"

Mama Buki's cheeks were wet as she kissed them. Sade clambered into the vehicle and crouched down in the narrow space. Femi followed and a few seconds later the blanket covered them like a great thunder cloud.

"Femi?" Sade whispered. "Are you all right?"

She stretched out her arm to touch her brother. Her fingers clasped something knobbly, his knee. Usually when they played in the dark it was a game, full of giggles and weird sounds intended to frighten each other. Now Femi made no response apart from a muffled sniff.

"Femi?" she repeated.

He jiggled his knee as if to shake her loose. Sade withdrew her hand and hugged herself tightly. She listened to Uncle Tunde open and close the trunk, climb into the front seat and slam the door. Each movement carried different vibrations. They were being swept away from their home and from Papa, submerged in darkness. The engine was revving now and they were leaving. To some unknown place. Only a few hours ago Mama had been carried away under a blinding-white sheet. Not seeing, not hearing, not feeling. But Sade could still hear and feel. She dug her fingers into her palms, wishing she could stop all sensation.

CHAPTER 4

"SO, YOU TWO WILL BE MY CHILDREN"

HUNCHED UNDER THE BLANKET, Sade heard Joseph clang the metal gates behind them, locking away the single-story white house in the compound that was home. Joseph had known them all their lives and they had not even said good-bye.

Sade tried to imagine what they were passing. Leaving. The avenue of palms and the giant-leafed plantains clustered at the corner. She and Femi used to believe that the street-ghosts hid behind them. Then Mr. Abiona's grocery table under the spidery almond tree, with tins, bottles, pots and boxes stacked high like colorful acrobats balancing on each other's shoulders. Whatever Mama ran out of—soap powder, matches, shampoo, palm oil—Mr. Abiona managed to produce it with a knowing smile. Sade would have liked to say good-bye to him too. She had seen him this morning, his cheeks squashed between his hands. His mouth open. Speechless. He was one of the first people to come running from outside . . . to see Mama lying in the driveway. He must have heard the shots. Perhaps he had even seen the gunman's car speeding away.

Already Femi was squirming, although the journey had

hardly even begun. Uncle Tunde was slowing the car down, stalling, turning a corner. They must be entering Adeniyi Jones Avenue, passing under the DR. MEYERS MILK OF MAGNESIA billboard. It was a joke between them to force each other to stretch their mouths wide open as they passed under the gigantic blue bottle tippling out its creamy contents. The dull drumming of traffic was now louder, punctured by sharp hoots, blasts and voices. They must have joined the streams of cars, trucks, motorcycles and cyclists thrusting their way to and from the city. Had they passed the trestle tables where Grandma's friend, Mama Lola, sat with her pyramids of oranges? Whenever Grandma came to stay, the two old ladies spent hours sitting there together, chatting in Yoruba about everything under the sun. In between, Mama Lola served her customers. They had been friends since childhood, but Mama Lola looked far more wrinkled, older and bent. "Poor Mama Lola," Grandma often said. Sorrow had entered her home like a thief in the night. Having lost every one of her children, she was forced to sell oranges to earn a living. But now Grandma had lost her own child too. Did she know yet? Who would tell her? Would Mama Buki have to carry the bitter words in her mouth? Grandma would surely know as soon as she saw Mama Buki. Sade could just imagine their grandmother's eyes misting over, her furrowed skin crumpling.

Whenever would they see Grandma again? Sade pressed her face against her knees, her body shaking with each jolt through the floor of the car. She and Femi were like two pebbles rattling in a tin, about to be flung away.

"Sade! Femi! Stay absolutely still! Police check!"

Uncle Tunde's voice was taut as the car slowed down. They had been going faster. They must have left the jostling city streets and were traveling on the open road out of Lagos. Femi's fingers grazed Sade's arm under the blanket. She grasped his hand. The engine rumbled as the car shuddered almost to a halt, then revved up again. The police must be letting them through. Femi pulled his hand away.

"Well, that's Number One!" muttered Uncle Tunde, like a grim sports commentator. But he was calmer than Papa would have been. Police were always setting up roadblocks and Papa's anger simmered like pepper soup. The last time he had driven them to Grandma's they had been stopped more than twenty times on the road to Ibadan. Sade and Femi played a game. Who could spot the naira note as the policeman's hand swept expertly past that of the driver in front? Mostly taxi drivers with minibuses full of passengers had to pay up. Usually the policemen stared rudely at Papa, sometimes demanding to know where he was going, but they never actually demanded money. Something in his manner must have warned them. But when Papa had driven on, his anger would erupt as he fumed about the daylight robbery of innocent people. Mama would place her hand gently on his shoulder.

"Don't give yourself a heart attack, Folarin. That would please them."

Mama. Mama under the bedspread with crimson-soaked flowers. Mama under the blinding-white sheet. Mama who read Papa's article out loud.

"Every day we are robbed under our own noses. And it's no use complaining to the police. Why? Because they are the robbers."

"Do you really think they will let you get away with this, Folarin?" Mama had said.

"The bully only gets away with it because others let him. They'll have to lock me up before they shut me up."

Yet Mama had never told him not to write.

Uncle Tunde was slowing down again.

"Don't move, children! This one has a torch."

The car lurched to a halt and Sade heard the window being rolled down. She held her breath and hoped Femi was doing the same.

"I'm late, officer. My mother is coming to the airport now. I must be the first one she sets her eyes on. You know how it is with mothers!" Uncle Tunde laughed lightly, his tone smooth and polite.

"Oga, open de door! Wetin you carry for back?" The policeman barked.

"Oh, it's only rubbish at the back, officer!" Their uncle's voice rose on the word "rubbish," as if enjoying a joke. "I threw the blanket on top so my mother won't complain that her son is untidy!"

"OK, OK. Carry on!" The policeman was impatient.

"Thank you, officer. Very understanding."

The engine stormed into life again.

As soon as they had left the roadblock behind, Uncle Tunde instructed them to throw off the blanket and to sit on the backseat.

26

"Did you give him money, Uncle?" Sade asked, her heart pumping rapidly.

"Never you mind. That could have been nasty! If he insisted on looking, we would have been in big, big trouble."

"He would think you were kidnapping us!" Femi muttered, sniffing. He brushed his arm across his eyes. Had he been crying? He wriggled on the seat, stretching his legs, and turned away from Sade.

The lights of Murtala Muhammed Airport sparkled in the distance. Usually it was exciting coming out to the airport, especially in the evening. The main building glittered in layers like an enormous ocean liner out in the middle of an indigo sea. Thousands of invisible messages could be shooting at any moment between the great funnel-shaped control tower and invisible planes somewhere up there in the sky. But tonight Sade felt none of that excitement, only her stomach twisted and knotted. At this moment, someone in the control tower was preparing to direct the plane that was going to carry her and Femi far away from home.

Even at night the car park was as busy and noisy as any street market. They joined a winding stream of cars that eased their way through the crowds, who were hustling back and forth with bags and boxes. Having found a parking space, Uncle Tunde told the children to wait. He would go first and find the agent and Mrs. Bankole.

"I don't want to go, Sade," Femi blurted, as Uncle Tunde merged into the shadows of the crowd. "If we run away now, we'll miss the plane! They can't make us go!" The gleam from passing headlights lit up little rivers of tears trickling down his cheeks.

"We can't do that, Femi! Papa doesn't want us to go—but it's best."

Femi snorted and started fiddling with the handle of the door.

"If you run away, Femi, Papa will have to go to the police and then they'll get him!"

Reluctantly Femi withdrew his hand. Sade's words subdued them both, as if another blanket had been thrown over them. In silence, they watched the currents of people swirling by.

When Uncle Tunde opened the door, a short woman with mango-shaped cheeks stood beside him. Her green headscarf and dress glinted in the beams from an overhead lamp.

"Come out, children. This is Mrs. Bankole."

"So, you two will be my children!" The lady formed a little smile with lips that glistened a deep purple. Mama never wore lipstick.

Mrs. Peacock! Sade thought. She imagined a fan of feathers swooping up behind the lady. She loved making up names for people and, normally, this would have been a joke to share with Femi. But Papa's words rang in her ears.

"Until you are safely there, your surname is 'Bankole' and you must only use the names in the passport."

Sade tried to force the fanciful picture from her mind as they stepped hesitantly out of the car.

Both children held back as Mrs. Bankole stretched out her hands. Her wrists jingled with gold bangles and her chubby fingers were heavily ringed. Her nails matched her purple lips.

"Oh but you have to look the part!" A man in a pale suit, with a pink handkerchief flowering out of the top pocket, emerged from behind the lady. His cream jacket bulged out well beyond his legs.

"If you look out of place that will make trouble for everyone, including your father." His eyes narrowed as if to pin them down. He spoke briskly and his words carried the jagged edges of a warning. He was clearly the man who had fixed this all. The agent.

"It's very true, children. I'm sure you understand!" Uncle Tunde's voice carried a touch of the urgent pleading that Sade had heard him use earlier with Papa. It was different from his ordinary voice and not at all like his "court voice" when Papa had taken her to see his older brother at work. They had sat in the gallery and Papa had explained how Uncle Tunde was pleading for his client to the judge. His words and manner had been so confident. But now, did she detect uncertainty— even a hint of desperation—behind his words?

"It's only for one night—until Mrs. Bankole hands you over to your Uncle Dele. Don't forget your bags at the back." Uncle Tunde turned away, almost brusquely, as if not to let them see the concern in his eyes.

Slipping on her rucksack, Sade saw her uncle draw Mr. Fix-It aside and hand him a fat envelope. With his back to passersby, and partly shielded by Uncle Tunde and the car, Mr. Fix-It rapidly began counting through the wad of naira notes. In the flickering light, his stout forefinger jiggled at the speed of a fox pawing back earth around a rabbit hole.

Once again, Mrs. Bankole held out her ringed fingers. This time, reluctantly, Sade and Femi each took a hand.

"You are now my daughter, Yemi," she confided to Sade. "She will be thirteen next month. The thirteenth of December. You will remember that?"

Sade did not reply. The lady's hand felt slightly damp and sweaty and Sade winced at the thought of touching any of her jewelery. Mama only wore one simple wedding ring.

"And—by good fortune—my ten-year-old son is the same age as your brother! So, young man, you are Ade—and your birthday is March the first. You had better learn that."

Femi looked as if he wanted to worm himself away. He glared at his feet. Even when Uncle Tunde said good-bye and promised that Papa would be with them soon, Femi refused to raise his head.

CHAPTER 5

SPINNING INTO DARKNESS

TWO POLICEMEN IN BLACK BERETS were chatting to each other at the entrance to Departures. One rested his hand on the gun tucked into his belt, his fingers drumming lightly on the handle. Mr. Fix-It had trundled Mrs. Bankole's large maroon suitcase behind them. He pushed it to her now. Mrs. Bankole juggled with a matching small maroon box and a mock leopard-skin coat.

"This is as far as I come," he said smoothly. "Have a very pleasant journey, Mrs. Bankole."

Then he beamed at the children.

"Well, Yemi and Ade!" he rolled their names loudly. "Be good now and make sure you don't give your mother any trouble!"

Mr. Fix-It extended his hand to pat each of them lightly on the head. Sade had to restrain herself from flinching as his fingers brushed her hair. She saw Femi jolt, gritting his teeth. But when she glanced at the policemen, they were still busy talking.

Inside the building, people in khaki uniforms with black berets were checking cases and tickets. But before they had even reached the queue, a figure in a sunny yellow *agbada* staggered backward, almost stumbling over Mrs. Bankole's suitcase. A man with a telephone held to one ear was kicking Mr. Sunny Yellow and swearing!

"Eh, eh, eh!" Mrs. Bankole's voice rose, but stopped swiftly. A large baton hung from the waist of the man with the telephone. Security! Mr. Sunny Yellow somehow swiveled upward in an arc, curved around and ran off. Jutting his jaw out scornfully, Mr. Security returned to his conversation.

When it came to their turn, Mrs. Bankole heaved the maroon suitcase on to the platform. Sade thrust their small brown holdall alongside it. Not bothering to compete with the surrounding noise, Black Beret pointed to Mrs. Bankole's case and imitated the turning of a key. He appeared bored as he observed her jeweled fingers struggle with the lock. But as soon as she pulled back the lid, he signed to her with a quick somersault of his hand. He wanted her to take everything out. Mrs. Bankole said nothing but slipped a bangled hand into the side of her case. Sade thought she glimpsed the corner of a naira note. After withdrawing her hand, Mrs. Bankole busied herself with her handbag. Sade watched the man's arm now slither like a snake down the same side of the suitcase. Then casually, he lifted a few clothes before indicating with a tiny jerk of his head that Mrs. Bankole could close the case. His closed palm wove its way skillfully into his trouser pocket and when his hand reappeared, it was open and signaled to the woman officer next to him. No words passed. She slapped labels on to both pieces of luggage. As if completing the silent dance, Black Beret and his companion swung the suitcase onto a conveyor belt behind them. The little brown bag followed and within seconds both had disappeared through a dark hole in the wall.

A narrow gate led to a couple of tall desks and more khaki uniforms. Three gleaming brass buttons crested the shoulder of the man waiting for them. Again no words were exchanged as Mrs. Bankole produced her passport. Brass Buttons's eyes rested briefly on each of them before dipping down to study the little book and his computer. Mrs. Bankole's glittery-green *buba* rose and fell steadfastly until Brass Buttons finally flashed back the passport, nodding them on.

"What's that?" Femi broke his silence. His eyebrows and forehead puckered with suspicion.

Ahead of them, a woman in a blue uniform was sweeping a thick black rod up and down people who had stepped through a metal door frame. It looked like some magic ritual.

"It's to stop people smuggling," Sade said.

"But we're being smuggled," Femi whispered fiercely in her ear.

Mrs. Bankole swung around, her face issuing a stern warning.

"Ade, my boy," she said. "Take off your rucksack. Put it there. For X-ray."

Femi folded his arms as if he hadn't heard.

"Please, F—!" Sade stopped herself. Right behind them stood a man in dark glasses. He was wearing a flowing white *agbada* with a pattern of staring jet-black eyes. Sade slipped off her own rucksack.

"Shall I help you, Ade?" she offered softly.

Femi swung the bag roughly off his back, just missing Sade before he slung it onto the conveyor belt. He was behaving like he did when he was overtired and no one could reason with him.

"Doesn't he want to go on a plane?" drawled Mr. Agbada Eyes. His accent was American and the question was addressed to Sade, but Mrs. Bankole quickly intervened.

"Children of nowadays! They take everything for granted!" she exclaimed. "Airplanes are like fast cars to them."

"Well, air power has sure helped make the world a smaller place. Just one big global village, ma'am!"

He swept a circle in the air with one arm, making the eyes on his *agbada* jiggle.

Once past the rod and the X-ray, Mrs. Bankole steered the children to a row of seats. Mr. Agbada Eyes followed them, keen to relate to Mrs. Bankole how this trip to Nigeria had been his lifetime ambition.

"Tracing my roots, ma'am! Finding out where we black folk in America come from, you might say!"

Mr. Agbada Eyes began to talk about stories of Africa that had been passed down through his granddaddy. Femi nudged Sade, pointing to the shops. Next to a window of cameras was an open kiosk with crocodile skins hanging down the side.

"Can . . . can we . . . look over there? We won't go far." Sade couldn't bring herself to say a word like "mother."

Mrs. Bankole hesitated, but Mr. Agbada Eyes laughed.

"Guess this old history is boring them!"

Mrs. Bankole's purple lips wavered before reminding them to stay in sight.

• • •

Femi wrinkled his nose in front of the baby crocodile hand-bag. Its flattened head with crazy-paving patterns and sad empty eyeholes formed the front flap.

"It's brutal! Killing a baby crocodile!" he announced, loudly enough for the kiosk lady to hear although she pretended not to. The lady smiled at Femi. Why did so many grown-ups pretend and lie? But not Papa. And that's why Mama was . . . Sade slammed down the shutter in her brain.

"I think it's horrible too," she replied clearly. Next to the crocodile bag were carvings of animals and a cluster of wooden heads. Many of the heads looked quite similar until she noticed the pair in the far corner. She studied the faces. The carved pattern of the woman's hair was so familiar. How like an older version of her own pair they were! Her own Oko and Iyawo . . . stranded . . . deserted . . . on her desk at home. Impulsive hot tears pricked and burned.

"I-I need the toilet," she managed to whisper.

Behind the closed door, Sade crouched on the seat trying to contain the waves of sobs. Her hands over her mouth did their best to stifle them. But she was trembling as badly as one of those lemons that hung on so desperately when Mama shook the branch. Pulling the chain, she tried to drown her strangled cries.

"Yemi! Hurry up now! They have announced our flight!" It was Mrs. Bankole, sharp as any peacock.

"I'm coming." Sade's lips mouthed the words.

"Yemi! Do you hear me? Yemi?"

Forcing her legs into action, Sade undid the lock.

"I felt sick," she mumbled feebly.

For Sade, much of the journey was a blur. It was unreal. Yesterday evening she had been at her desk doing her homework. Like any other school night. Mama bringing her a chocolate drink before she went to bed, telling her that she shouldn't stay up too late. Don't worry, Mama, she had replied, Iyawo is watching. It was a joke between them. That Oko and Iyawo kept an eye on her for Papa and Mama.

But, tonight . . . What was she doing looking at those rows of wooden heads in an airport kiosk instead of at her own Oko and Iyawo? Who was this stranger, calling her Yemi, pretending to be their mother? Was this just a nightmare? Perhaps she would wake up in her own bed with Mama shaking her gently. "What's wrong, my child?" she would ask. "A bad dream?"

Sade was vaguely aware of the flight attendant giving instructions about lifebelts and oxygen masks, of Femi fiddling with earphones and buttons, of roaring in her ears while she peered out into the night where shadowy shapes fell away beneath them. Somewhere, already far below, giant-leafed plantains were whispering under the lamplight at the corner and Mr. Abiona's old wooden table was tucked away for the night underneath the almond tree. Somewhere, casuarina pines were spreading their needle-fine fingers against the sky and sending their scent into an empty room where a wooden girl with patterned hair watched over a vacant desk. But below them, all that could now be seen through the plane window was a scattering of pinprick lights surrounded by darkness. Soon those too had become fainter until there was nothing.

It had been one of Sade's dreams to travel on an airplane. Papa and Mama had promised they would take them one day. But it was not meant to be like this. Tonight she was spinning into the darkness of space, let loose from almost everything and everyone she knew, except Femi. And he too was slipping from her fingers.

CHAPTER 6

FLIGHT

"ARE YOUR CHILDREN ALL RIGHT?"

The blue-button eyes of the flight attendant startled Sade. They darted between the children and Mrs. Bankole. Neither Sade nor Femi had touched anything on the plastic trays of food.

"Thank you. They're just tired!"

Mrs. Bankole and the flight attendant smiled at each other. Sade and Femi remained silent. On a screen above them, a tiny stick-insect plane perched over a map of Africa, pointing northwards over the Sahara. A loudspeaker voice gave details of how high . . . far . . . fast they were traveling. Every hour that little black fly-thing would show them being carried more and more hundreds of miles away from home.

Sade pulled down the window shutter, then closed her eyes, trying to shut everything out. But there was no escape from the steady booming of the engines as she fell in and out of fitful bouts of sleep. At one point, Mama was squeezing the children's hands as she led them along a deep forest path. Slits of light filtered through the spiked leaves of giant palms. But when they came to a clearing and Sade looked up at

Mama, she found herself looking at an unknown woman's face. Another time, Sade was struggling to stay close to Mama among the crowd streaming through the narrow alleys of Alade Market. Mama had picked up a small saucer of buttons and was holding up a dazzling blue button to the light, asking "Will this color do?" Sade stretched out her hand to take the button but the whole saucer was sent flying as some men in white robes suddenly pushed past them. Sade woke up clutching her fists, straining against the seatbelt. The cold air had crept under her blanket, through her thin sweater and jeans. Apart from the deep droning of the engines there were no other sounds. All the cabin lights were dimmed. Femi was curled up like a bundle underneath his blanket. Sade couldn't tell if he was actually asleep, but Mrs. Bankole certainly was, judging from her snores.

Sade shut her eyes again, trying to doze. But the whale-like monster that had swallowed them continued to roar as it winged its way over the earth. There was nothing they could do. Mama couldn't do anything, lying on the ground covered in a white sheet stained with crimson. And Papa couldn't do anything, kneeling next to her, crying.

In the morning when they opened the window shutter, the sky outside was streaked with colors of the rainbow. One minute it was shaded dark indigo blue to creamy white. The next minute, milky blue stretched toward a horizon of oranges and reds. Seconds later all they could see were mountains and valleys of fluffy white clouds.

"Maybe it's like snow," Femi whispered.

"Cotton wool!" Sade murmured.

For a short while they were absorbed in the strange sky outside until the flight attendant arrived with more trays of food. Sade felt little cramps in her stomach, but this time both she and Femi opened and sampled the parcels of food. Their last proper meal was one Mama had made for them.

The plane began to descend through clouds, revealing patchworks of fields from lime greens to chocolate browns. But the colors seemed drained of brightness and soon even those were lost in a hazy mist. When it lifted it was as if a wizard had changed the fields into thousands upon thousands of buildings as far as the eye could see. Everything seemed tinged with gray ash. So this was London and Uncle Dele must be down there, waiting for them. Far below them a river curled through the city like a giant brown python, swollen from overeating.

"Temperature in London today is eight degrees Celsius . . ."

Perhaps Uncle Dele would bring something warm for them to wear. Their cotton coats would certainly not be enough. Sade shivered.

CHAPTER 7

LONDON, ENGLAND

NOTHING TO DECLARE

"DON'T SPEAK UNLESS YOU HAVE TO," Mrs. Bankole warned them. She had smiled good-bye to the flight attendant, but her fleshy cheeks now seemed to stiffen at the corners of her mouth. Mrs. Bankole lowered her voice despite the clatter of feet and squeaking of luggage wheels along a corridor that seemed to have no end. Sade read Femi's sullen face. Who would they want to speak to anyway? To say what? It was going to be difficult enough talking to Uncle Dele. Sade hoped Uncle Tunde had done all the explaining on the telephone and that he wouldn't ask more questions. How could she ever put the terrible pictures in her head into words?

"Hi there! Ain't you kids gonna freeze?"

It was the American. The black eyes on his outfit now peeped out from beneath a great black coat that matched a wide-brimmed felt hat.

"Oh, they'll be fine!" Mrs. Bankole replied quickly. "My brother will bring their winter coats to the airport. You know they don't feel the cold like me with my old bones!"

She laughed lightly and pretended to quiver a little underneath her own mock leopard-skin coat. The American glanced curiously at the children.

"Uh-huh? Well, have a good time!"

Neither Sade nor Femi said anything. He looked a little puzzled. With large strides, however, he was soon well in front of them.

At Immigration Control everyone came to a halt. Most of the passengers joined a long winding queue underneath a bright yellow sign with the words OTHER PASSPORTS in thick black letters. Mrs. Bankole shepherded the children into another shorter queue marked EUROPEAN COMMUNITY PASS- PORTS. It was moving more rapidly. Sade saw the American, near the back of the long queue, staring across at them. She shifted her gaze to the desks ahead of them at each of which perched a figure in a dark suit.

"Yemi, take this! Ade, come!" Mrs. Bankole thrust her small case into Sade's hand and led them up to the box. Mrs. Bankole held out her passport. In silence The Eyes behind the desk traveled down to the book, then sideways. Sade could just see the top of a computer. The Eyes suddenly flicked back to them, resting briefly on each in turn. As if taking three snapshots. Sade's stomach tightened and for the first time she began to worry about the passport. The Eyes were taking much longer than the Brass Buttons. Everyone else in this queue had gone through so quickly. What would happen if she and Femi were questioned? It wouldn't take long before the truth came out. And then? What if they were put on the next plane going home? The Eyes would tell the police in Lagos. Perhaps the police would try to use the children to get Papa . . .

Femi was fidgeting, stubbing one sneaker against the floor. Mrs. Bankole looked at him sharply. Sade wished she could send a message into his mind of what the Eyes could do. He shouldn't draw their attention. But Femi seemed in his own world. One hand on Mrs. Bankole's case, he swiveled around as if suddenly changing direction with a football.

"Ade!" Mrs. Bankole's voice carried a lightning warning.

Suddenly the Eyes relaxed.

"Practicing for the World Cup is he?" the man said, handing back the passport.

"Oh thank you, officer!" Mrs. Bankole's face lit up, storm avoided.

Sade was surprised by her own little leaps of relief.

A ramp led down to Baggage Reclaim. Suitcases, boxes and bags were lunging out on to conveyor belts that circled through the large hall. People crowded close, grabbing cases, pulling and pushing trolleys. It was not long before the little brown holdall was flung out on to the conveyor belt followed by Mrs. Bankole's large maroon suitcase.

Fastening the buttons of her shiny leopard-skin coat, Mrs. Bankole led the way underneath a green NOTHING TO DECLARE sign. Sade pushed the trolley with Femi dragging his feet beside her. Ahead of them, a small group of men and women stood in white shirts and black trousers beside a row of empty tables. Beyond was a large doorway. Was Uncle Dele waiting outside there, scanning all the faces? Just like they used to do in Lagos, when they went to the airport with Mama and Papa. But these buildings seemed even more enormous.

43

What if he was waiting somewhere else? How would they find him?

They were almost by the door when a voice stopped them.

"Over here, please!"

A short woman by the tables beckoned them. She had pepper-red lips and a bob of cassava yellow hair.

"I would like you to open your cases, madam."

Femi stepped closer to Sade, suddenly showing interest.

"But—I have nothing to declare," Mrs. Bankole said with determination.

Sade remembered Black Beret the night before and how Mrs. Bankole had managed to avoid unpacking everything.

"I want you to open your cases please, madam," Pepper-Red Lips repeated. This time Sade heard her stress the word "cases." The lady wanted to check their small brown bag as well.

Mrs. Bankole was about to heave the large suitcase onto the table when a man with a face as stiff and sharp as a rock hurried across to Pepper-Red Lips. He whispered something in her ear.

"Please follow us and bring your luggage with you," Pepper-Red Lips said quietly.

Sade saw Mrs. Bankole hesitate for a second. Then, drawing back her shoulders, she raised her head and stretched her neck proudly. A peacock preparing for a fight. She was as short as Pepper-Red Lips but her green headdress gave her a couple of extra inches.

"Why do you ask me this? What's going on here?" she

44

demanded, her tone rising boldly.

"We are Customs Officers, madam," answered Rock Face. Hardly a muscle moved in his face. He kept his voice down. "We are empowered to examine your goods. By law you are—"

"All right, all right!" Mrs. Bankole threw up her hands. "Do your work but just hurry up! My husband is waiting for me."

Sade and Femi glanced at each other. Mrs. Bankole had said nothing to them about her husband.

Rock Face unpacked and Pepper-Red Lips examined. As the stacks of brightly colored material next to the maroon suitcase grew taller, Sade thought of stalls in Alade Market. Almost thirty *bubas* with matching wraps and headscarves. A small mountain of decorated leather sandals. A mound of carved bracelets and gold bangles. Everything looked new. At least Pepper-Red Lips worked neatly. Not like the swarm of police who had tipped out Papa's suitcase when they had seized his passport. But Pepper-Red Lips seemed to be looking for something well hidden. When she came to Mrs. Bankole's toilet bag, she smelled and touched the contents of each jar . . . and suddenly Sade realized what they were after. Of course. Drugs! She had heard Papa and Mama talking about drug smuggling; how poor people could be tempted by the money. Papa had written some articles. Did Mrs. Bankole smuggle drugs as well as children? She didn't look very poor. Whatever would happen to them if Pepper-Red Lips found anything? Surely Uncle Tunde wouldn't have let them go with Mrs. Bankole if he thought she was a drug smuggler?

Nervously Sade chewed her thumb, watching the officers work in silence while Mrs. Bankole sat with her arms folded grimly.

"What are you going to do with these? Sell them?" The suitcase was empty at last and Pepper-Red Lips stood in front of Mrs. Bankole's goods.

"They are presents." Mrs. Bankole waved a hand as if swatting a fly. "For family, friends . . . everyone likes to have something from home."

Pepper-Red Lips raised her eyebrows.

"You have rather a lot of family and friends, don't you think?"

Before Mrs. Bankole could reply, Rock Face pointed to the brown holdall.

"Did you pack this yourself?" he asked smoothly.

"The children did," Mrs. Bankole replied.

"We still need to check it," he said.

Sade slipped her arm around Femi and he didn't push it away.

"Uncle Dele's waiting for us!" he muttered so that only his sister could hear.

Their small bundle of clothes looked odd next to Mrs. Bankole's stacks. Wouldn't the officers wonder about the oddness? But, no . . . Pepper-Red Lips was showing interest in Sade's gold thread *aso-oke*. She examined the small matching blue bag, pressing the padded satin lining between her fingers. She handed it to Rock Face and his thick fingers began to crawl all over it. Sade wanted to shout at them, grab it away. It was her bag! The one Mama had sewn specially for her. The only thing she had of Mama's now.

She swallowed her words, keeping her lips pressed tight. But when Pepper-Red Lips flashed out a pair of small scissors from her pocket to snip at the seams, Sade couldn't stop herself.

"No!" she cried. "Don't cut it! Please!"

Mrs. Bankole shot out her arm to hold Sade back.

"You people have seen everything already. What are you doing now?"

"Parents sometimes use their children to carry illegal substances," Rock Face stated bluntly. "If you have nothing to hide, you have nothing to fear."

Sade trembled and forced herself to watch as Pepper-Red Lips cut the threads that Mama had sewn with so much skill and love.

It was another hour before Pepper-Red Lips and Rock Face let them go. They had found no drugs but insisted that Mrs. Bankole pay import duty on the other things. She argued loudly but, in the end, she paid. When, at last, Sade and Femi trailed behind her into the Arrivals Hall, there was no sign of Uncle Dele anywhere.

CHAPTER 8

VICTORIA STATION

VICTORIA . . . VICTORIA . . . Sade repeated the name to herself of the station where Mrs. Bankole said they would get off. Buildings, streets, roofs, telephone wires, trees, cloudy sky and now dirty tunnel walls hurtled by outside the train window. Inside the compartment, the passengers reminded Sade of a page in her children's encyclopedia illustrating people from all around the world. A map above the opposite seats showed a long blue line, looped at one end with a picture of an airplane. Little squares and circles, each with a name, were dotted along its length. So many different stations! Another map showed many different colored lines, weaving in and out of each other, and dozens of other stations. It would be so easy to get lost. Why hadn't Uncle Dele come to meet them in this gigantic city? Sade felt her stomach encircled and twisted by a web of ever-tightening wire.

The trouble at Customs had clearly upset Mrs. Bankole. She was also clearly annoyed not to find their uncle at the airport. Now she would have to take the children to Uncle Dele's college. There had also been no sign of a "Mr. Bankole." Mrs. Bankole did not mention him again but began to grouse about having to drag all her baggage around London. It seemed that she meant the children too.

Waiting for the train, a little distance from the other passengers, she had whispered a strong warning. On no account were the children to tell anyone her name. Ever. Even if they were made to admit that they had entered the country by pretending to be someone else's children. She threatened that if they ever mentioned her name, the agent who had helped them in Lagos would hear about it. Then he would never help their father and Papa would not be able to join them.

Throughout the journey Mrs. Bankole was silent, except when they changed trains from the map's blue line to the green and she told them to stay close. At Victoria, Sade helped push the large maroon suitcase onto the platform, then hurried to keep up as Mrs. Bankole pulled the case behind her. Femi tagged farther behind with the brown holdall.

"Be quick! Those airport people made us late," Mrs. Bankole said forcefully. "I have to meet someone before we take the thirty-six to your uncle."

Sade noticed that Mrs. Bankole no longer called them "Yemi" and "Ade."

Mrs. Bankole steered her way through the crowd, up stairs, escalators and along winding corridors to the ticket machine. A metal bar lifted to let each of them out.

"Hurry now!" Mrs. Bankole rushed on, leading them into an area of shops and stalls, all under a vast roof. Turning the corner they almost tripped over a young man sharing a sleeping bag with a dog. Both the man and the dog had narrow, pointed faces and startled eyes.

"Can you spare any change?" the man asked. Mrs. Bankole ignored him. People were hurrying in all directions while others stood staring up at an enormous notice board. Mrs. Bankole headed toward a cafe.

"Oh, he's still there!" She sounded relieved. "Wait here, you two!"

A large, heavily built man was just coming out of the cafe entrance, making his way between the tables outside. Mrs. Bankole hurried toward him. Before he had even opened his mouth, he looked fierce. His face was square with his hair cut as level as a table, descending to a flattened U shape on his forehead.

"Where have you been? I had to ring the airport so many times! Your plane landed nearly four hours ago!" he said angrily. Sade could tell from his accent he was Nigerian. Was this Mr. Bankole?

"The problem was in Customs! It's not my fault!" Mrs. Bankole retorted. "We were stopped."

"We?"

Mrs. Bankole hesitated.

"Let me get these children something to drink first," she said. "Then I'll explain."

The man stared at them, scowling.

"Children? Whose children?"

"I said that I will explain in a minute."

"What have you got yourself into? Are you mad?"

Mrs. Bankole grabbed Sade's hand and thrust some coins into it. She pointed to the counter inside the cafe.

"Get something. I'll come soon."

Without giving them time to reply, she pushed them through the door and hurried back outside. Femi pulled a face and made his way to the counter.

"Coke, please, and one of those," he said to a pink-cheeked woman with a white cap. He pointed to a square of chocolate cake.

"The same please," added Sade.

As soon as the words were out, she realized she should first check that the five coins in her hand would be enough. But before she could say anything, the white-capped woman had turned her back and was already pressing a lever on a machine and briskly pouring their drinks.

"Four twenty," she said, sweeping two plates of chocolate cake on to the counter. Hiding her nervousness, Sade offered all five coins and watched the pink fingers dance across the buttons on the till. Without looking at the children, the woman slapped four small silver coins back on to the counter.

They carried their drinks and plates to a table. When Mama or Papa had taken them to eat out at home, the waiters often talked and joked with them.

"Machine Lady!" Sade whispered to Femi but he was too busy burrowing into his cake to reply.

Outside the cafe, Mrs. Bankole and Mr. Bad Temper had moved a little farther away from the cafe door and were standing in front of a flower stall. If this was Mr. Bankole, he didn't look at all happy at seeing his wife again. Sade couldn't hear what they were saying but from their expressions and hands, it appeared they were still arguing. At times, Mrs. Bankole glanced uneasily across at the cafe.

"Sade?" Femi had finished his cake and most of his drink when he paused to look up at his sister. "Why do you think Uncle Dele didn't come to the airport?" His voice was small.

The criss-cross wire around Sade's stomach tightened. Perhaps the panicky flutterings showed on her face because Femi quickly changed the subject.

"Let me see their money," he said, stretching out his hand.

Sade passed him a small silver coin. She examined one herself, running her forefinger around the edges. It was almost round but had little corners.

"She's their queen," said Femi.

On the other side was a rose with a crown.

"It says 'twenty pence,'" said Sade. "So we've got eighty. I'm sure she'll want them back."

But when Sade looked up in the direction of the flower stall, the place where Mrs. Bankole had been standing with Mr. Bad Temper was empty.

CHAPTER 9

WHERE IS UNCLE DELE?

GRABBING THEIR RUCKSACKS and the brown holdall, they bolted out of the cafe. They stood for a few seconds outside the door, scanning the crowds. Mrs. Bankole was nowhere to be seen. They ran to the flower stall, stopped and turned in every direction. No sign at all.

"What shall we do, Sade?" Femi's eyes looked as bewildered as Grandma's young goats when he chased them.

"Let's wait a little in the cafe. Perhaps she has just gone somewhere for a few minutes." Sade spoke without believing her own words.

Machine Lady was clearing away their table when they returned. There was still a little Coke in each of their glasses.

"I thought you had left," she said bluntly.

Sade shook her head and Machine Lady shoved the glasses back onto the table.

The children sipped their drinks slowly, not wanting to reach the final drops. Both sat facing the window, their eyes constantly darting back to the clock as if, by magic, Mrs. Bankole might suddenly reappear. Neither wanted to move, although somewhere deep inside herself Sade sensed that

Mrs. Bankole had really left them. The piece of paper on which Papa had written the details of Uncle Dele's college had gone with her. Mrs. Bankole had asked to see it when they were on the train and had put it into her bag.

"Do you want to order anything else?" Machine Lady's voice was sharp. They had been sitting at the table for a while. Sade and Femi shook their heads.

"Well, this isn't a waiting room! If you're waiting for somebody, you need the waiting room."

Unwillingly they slung their rucksacks on to their backs.

"It's not even full," grumbled Femi, loud enough for Machine Lady to hear as he picked up the holdall.

Keeping close to each other, they wandered through the station. It had been possible to ignore the wintry air while they had been rushing behind Mrs. Bankole or had been protected in the train and the cafe. But now the chill seeped through their flimsy cotton coats, down to their bones. Sharp gusts of even colder air struck them as they reached a large archway leading to the street. It felt like they were stepping into a thousand-piece jigsaw puzzle. Sade grasped Femi's hand and leaned against a shop window to keep out of the stream of passersby. Lagos was full of huge buildings but they were surrounded by light, air and space. Here each was packed up against the next. Together they loomed over the narrow pavements like a thick forest of brick, concrete and glass.

"What if we can't find Uncle Dele?" Femi tugged her hand. His voice had the whine he used with Mama.

"Papa told us where he works. We'll find the place." Sade tried to sound confident.

At least she remembered the name of the college. She could see the letters as Papa had printed them. LONDON COL-LEGE OF ART. But nothing else. She wondered if they should try stopping someone to ask. After Machine Lady in the cafe, she didn't really fancy that. From her pocket she pulled out the four coins to check they were still there.

"We have to take a bus," Sade added. "What did Mrs. Bankole say? Thirty something?"

Femi looked blank.

Two red double-decker buses, one behind the other, trundled around the corner. They watched them draw to a halt farther down the road. Was that perhaps their direction? Then another red bus rumbled by, this time without turning the corner. Or was that their direction? Or was it the oppo-site way? If only there was some clue. A bus approached them with a sign above the front window that said BRIGHTON.

"Brighton Rangers, Sade!" called Femi.

She couldn't help smiling. Anything to do with English football, Femi knew about it. Uncle Dele had sent him a book on English football clubs, so he knew all about them too.

Together they began to read the place names on the buses and Femi nudged Sade whenever he recognized one from his book. Queens Park, Crystal Palace . . . But, of course, none of the buses or coaches carried a sign for LONDON COLLEGE OF ART.

And the more place names they read, the more frightened Sade felt. The eighty pence in her pocket could not be worth very much at all. Would it even buy them a bus ticket each? They could not afford to take the wrong bus and these buses seemed to be going to dozens of different places.

Sade was beginning to recognize the numbers. A 36 passed followed by a 38. She was almost sure that Mrs. Bankole had said one of those. If only she had paid more attention.

"We'll have to ask," she said to Femi.

Most of the passersby kept their eyes fixed ahead as if intent on reaching some distant point. Sade hesitated, gathering courage to stop someone. She swallowed, trying to prepare her words. If she couldn't catch someone's eye, she would have to catch their attention some other way. A lady in a long black coat and a smart black turban-shaped hat was coming toward them. Her high heels seemed to make her walk a little more slowly than everyone else. Sade stepped forward.

"Excuse me, please—" But before she could even ask her question, the lady pulled away. Her gloved hand shot up as if to ward Sade off.

"No. No, thank you!" The words shot out. The lady did not even look at Sade as she scuttled by. Sade edged back, astonished. It was like having a door slammed in her face.

"So rude!" Femi exclaimed.

The lady had treated her like a beggar! What was that saying of Mama's?

A beggar must be prepared to wait.

But this was even more horrible! Did Mrs. Gloved Hands think she would catch a disease if she spoke to them? And they weren't begging! All they wanted was to know the way to Uncle Dele's college.

"Try him, Sade!" Femi indicated a man carrying a briefcase.

Sade took a deep breath and started again. No one else pulled away but most of the replies were brisk. No. Sorry. Never heard of it. Don't know, love. Others just shook their heads. She was beginning to despair when someone said, "Can I help you?"

A young man with a rucksack slung over his shoulder had overheard her question and stopped. If the long twists of corn-colored hair that hung down to his shoulders had been darker, they would have suited an egungun mask.

"Take the thirty-six, just down there," he said. "Ask the bus driver to tell you when to get off. College is on the main road. You can't miss it."

"Thank you," replied Sade. She tried to return the young man's smile but her face felt quite stiff with the cold.

The number 36 bus driver's eyes were also friendly. He looked as if he could be Nigerian, thought Sade, until he repeated her words in an accent she did not recognize. His words rose upward, as if they might fly away into a song.

"You want the College of Art? They take students so young these days?"

He laughed at his own joke as he slid their four coins into a machine that rolled out a ticket strip. It was exactly the right money, no change. Sade gripped the metal pole.

"Can you tell us when we get there, please?" she asked. It was an effort to keep her voice steady.

"Jus' leave it to me!" he replied, shifting back to his

steering wheel and revving the engine.

Soon they were traveling over a large bridge. For a few seconds they glimpsed a postcard view of London up the river. Like the one Uncle Dele had sent them. Big Ben above the Houses of Parliament. They had placed the card on the sideboard next to the small chrome and black radio on which Papa listened every morning at breakfast to the BBC World Service broadcasting from London. It became a family joke that the BBC controlled Papa and breakfast. Everyone had to be quiet. Mama would put her finger to her lips if Sade or Femi started to talk. It had been like that only yesterday morning. Before their world had turned upside down. Before they had been propelled to this other side of the world. Now here they were on a bus just a bridge away from Big Ben itself. Thousands of miles away from home . . . from Papa, Uncle Tunde, Mama Buki . . . Grandma and all the family . . . and, most terrible of all, from Mama . . . forever and ever. Never again would Mama be able to tell them to be quiet so that Papa could listen to his news from London. Never. Nothing made sense except the terrible aching inside Sade. Certainly none of the images that slid across the window screen outside the bus made any sense. The things she saw might just as well be cardboard cutouts on a film set that they had entered by mistake. The problem was that there was no exit.

But now they were on their way to Uncle Dele and at least he was one person who came from their real world. He would take care of them.

"London College of Art!" the driver almost sang.

Sade and Femi stepped down from the bus. In front of them rows of gray stone steps led up to large glass doors. Behind a ground-level window, some students sat at long tables working on small clay sculptures. Carrying the holdall between them, they climbed up to the entrance and pushed open the heavy glass door.

"Can I help you?" The face of the lady behind the counter was neatly framed by silky brown hair.

"We are looking for Doctor Dele Ṣolaja, please." Sade tried hard to appear poised.

"Is he expecting you?"

"We don't know," blurted Femi.

Miss Silky Neat looked curiously at them.

"I haven't actually seen him come in today. In fact I haven't seen him for a while. But I'll try his department for you," she said, picking up the telephone.

Miss Silky Neat lowered her voice but the entrance hall was quiet and they could hear everything she said.

"Oh? For a whole week, you say? . . . No, I thought I hadn't seen him for a few days . . . Oh dear! . . . The police? What have they said? . . ."

Silent and horrified, the children waited for her to finish and explain. Miss Silky Neat put the telphone down. For a couple of seconds her face was strangely flustered, before she composed it again.

"Dr. Ṣolaja hasn't been in for the last week, I'm afraid."

"Where is he?" Sade asked boldly.

"Well, he hasn't rung and apparently there has been no reply from his flat for the whole week. It's so unlike him. I am told that the police are following it up."

Sade and Femi glanced anxiously at each other. The lady inspected them again with a new curiosity.

"How do you know Doctor Solaja? Is he a friend—or a relative?"

"He's our—" Femi began.

"Friend—a friend of the family," Sade interrupted. "Can we have his address?"

"We don't give out personal information about staff. But perhaps you should see someone from the department." She leaned forward, frowning slightly. "You might have some information that could be useful to the police."

"We have to go, thank you," announced Sade quickly.

Before Miss Silky Neat could say any more, Sade had turned around with Femi in tow. Struggling with the holdall, they heaved open the heavy glass door. Only when they reached the bottom of the steps and were out of view did they stop. They stood shivering beneath the lifeless branches of a bare tree while the chilly afternoon air wound long shadowy fingers around them. Ahead of them, the khaki-gray mottled bark of the trees lining the road reminded Sade of a row of soldiers in camouflage.

"I want Papa . . . and Mama!" Femi whimpered.

Sade put her arm around him. The tears she wanted to cry were frozen.

CHAPTER 10

THIEVES AND VANDALS

IT WAS BETTER TO KEEP WALKING. Try to find somewhere they could shelter. The clock in the college had said half-past four but the sky was darkening fast. Lights now glittered everywhere. Splashes of yellow from streetlamps, car headlights, buses with windows ablaze and shops with neon signs replaced the dull grays of the day. They kept to the main road. There were so many side roads, most of them smaller and quieter. Never would they have been allowed to go wandering alone like this in Lagos. Yet here they were, in another great sprawling city, with absolutely no idea of where they were, nor of where they were going. With Uncle Dele missing, they were now completely and utterly alone. If anyone asked where they came from and what they were doing, whatever should they say? How could they explain what they were doing here, two children alone, in London? Two children who were not meant to be here . . . who had tricked the Eyes at the airport. Even thinking about the questions they would be asked was too frightening.

It seemed to Sade that they had been walking for miles. Femi began to straggle behind.

"Where are we going, Sade?" he groaned.

"I don't know," she said. "Maybe we'll find somewhere."

Whenever they stopped, the icy wind speared even more fiercely through their thin layers of cotton. Other people wore thick coats, many with hats, scarves and gloves. Everyone seemed in a hurry. Probably they were already on their way home for the evening. No one took any notice of them. It was as if they were invisible.

They reached another row of shops. Femi tugged at his handle of the holdall.

"Do you smell that, Sade?"

Her brother pulled her toward the smell of frying fish. She was hungry now as well. In a shop with plate glass across the whole frontage, people were queueing at a long white counter. A man with a white cap was shaking a basket of chips. There was no point waiting and looking—it only made the hunger worse. But when, a little farther along, they came to a cafe with red checked curtains and matching tablecloths, they stopped to stare inside. A waiter was serving two platefuls of what looked like rice and stew to a couple sitting by the window. When the waiter looked up, he frowned and shook his head at them. Embarrassed, they turned away. A customer opened the cafe door and a gust of warm air brushed past them. A second later the warmth and scents had vanished. How long could they manage like this with no money and no food?

It was when, however, they came to a shop with plantains and yams piled up by the doorway and windows heaped with bags of rice and gari, that they could not resist going in. The shop smelled of Lagos. Spices, oils, dried fish and fresh vegetables were all crammed onto overflowing shelves. Bottles and tins did extraordinary balancing acts like on Mr. Abiona's stall.

"Plantain chips!" Femi whispered.

He picked up a cellophane packet, brought it up close to his face and sniffed it before slowly replacing it. They walked through the shop, squeezing past a couple of other customers in the narrow passages. They took their time examining items on each side. After circling twice, they still wanted to delay returning outside into the biting wind. But the man behind the counter had become suspicious.

"What is it you children want?" he demanded.

Sade and Femi hesitated.

"If you are just waiting for someone, then wait outside, please," he stated in a no-nonsense tone. Sade felt blood rush to her face. He thought they were thieves! Of course she and Femi wanted something . . . something to eat! But they could hardly say, "We'd like some plantain chips please but we have no money."

Femi responded before Sade.

"This food isn't good. Not like in Lagos!" he said loudly. "Come on, Sade, we'll go to another shop!"

They resettled their rucksacks and pulled back their shoulders before walking out. Neither of them looked in the direction of the counter but a lady's voice followed them.

"Makes you wonder about some parents, doesn't it, Mr. Mills?"

Cars were still streaming along the road but fewer people

were out walking now. They needed to find a place where they could at least huddle up together and try to keep each other warm. Somewhere near light, but also hidden. The small towels Mama Buki had packed for them in their holdall could be their blankets. They began looking for a shop entrance set back from the pavement that did not have a metal grille blocking it. When they came to the corner of one of the darker side roads, they hesitated. Perhaps there might be somewhere there? But it seemed quite deserted and more frightening. They carried on.

In the next block, Femi pulled Sade to a halt next to a narrow alleyway between two buildings.

"I can't walk any more!" Femi's voice quavered.

Sade peered into the alleyway. It was too murky to see beyond the entrance. The damp smell was like the open drains in Alade Market after a downpour. It would be horrible to spend a night in there. But before she could say anything, Femi thrust down the holdall just inside the alley and curled himself up like a snail on top of it.

"Femi, please—" Sade began. She broke off in horror as a shape rose up from the deeper shadows of the alley.

"Clear off! This place is mine!"

Femi sprung up wildly, colliding into Sade. The man's arm swept down toward their bag and snatched it.

"I said clear off! Everything here is mine!" he growled like an old lion defending his den. His eyes were concealed under a hat but they had heard enough. There was not the slightest chance of retrieving their bag. They fled.

Rucksacks bumping on their backs, they kept running.

The man stayed in his alley but the terror followed them as they ran along a dimly lit parade. They were both panting by the time they reached the only brightly lit shop. It displayed posters of videos and a large sign saying OPEN UNTIL 11 P.M.! Breathing heavily, they pushed open the glass door and made for a corner as far as possible from the counter. For a minute or so they stood rooted to the floor, trying to calm down. Around them were shelves of videos. Instead of James Bond, Superman or any other video star, however, Sade still saw the terrifying Darth Vader of the alley looming up above them, his arm sweeping away their holdall. What would he do with their clothes? What would he do with the beautiful *aso-oke* Mama had made for her with its own matching bag? A bag with a broken lining. Mama's present had barely survived the customs officer's scissors only to be seized by a stranger in a stinking alley. What kind of place had they come to?

Femi dug Sade in the ribs and jutted his chin toward the back of the shop. A man was eyeing them from behind the counter.

"Can I help you?" he asked loudly. He didn't sound as if he wanted to be helpful. Sade pursed her lips together. What could she say? The kind of help they needed was impossible. Mama would have understood how hopeless it was. She would have summed it up with one of her proverbs.

Even the best cooking pot will not produce food by itself.

Of course they needed help!

"I said, can I help you?" Video Man repeated, a little more loudly and abruptly. Sade lingered a few seconds before extending her hand to her brother.

"Come on, Femi," she murmured and turned toward the door. But at that moment the door was flung open and four boys with dark glasses and woolly hats pulled down low over their foreheads burst inside. Shouting and swearing, they sent video boxes flying off the shelves, then kicked the stands. Sade and Femi cowered back into the corner. The boys ignored them. Two of them ripped the posters from the window alongside the children. Laughing, they tore them into pieces. Video Man grabbed his telephone. He rasped out a message to the police. But as soon as he had slammed down the receiver and lifted the counter bar to chase his intruders, they darted back out into the street.

"That'll teach you to mess with our mates!" the last one to leave yelled at Video Man. He punched the air as if they had just scored a goal. Seconds later a sharp crack shattered the front window. Sade and Femi had remained riveted in their corner, almost in a stupor. First Darth Vader of the alley, now this! But the sound of the crack, followed by glass splintering, sent Sade's mind spinning.

Grabbing Femi's hand, she bolted toward the door. They had to be well out of the way when the police came. But Video Man got there before them and thrust his key into the lock.

"Don't think you're getting away with this!" he puffed grimly. His face glowed a furious red.

"I know how you kids work together! Sent you in as decoys, didn't they? Distracting me, so I didn't see 'em coming! Well, you can tell your story to the police!"

CHAPTER 11

POLICE BUSINESS AND COOL GAZE

THERE IS A GREAT BANGING *and rattling on the iron gates. They have finished eating dinner and are watching television. Papa hurries to the window, draws back the curtain just a little and peers out through the bars on the window. The sky is dark but lights are flashing above the gates.*

"Police! Police! Open de door! Open de door! I say open de door!"

"Oh my God! What have they come for now, Folarin?" *Mama runs across the sitting room and puts out her hand to grip Papa's shoulder.*

"Open am! Open am! Or we go break dis gate o!"

Papa calls to Joseph. The young man runs and Papa strides across the drive to the gate. Sade and Femi watch from inside next to Mama. She has an arm around each of them. They are silent and tense.

"I want proof of your identity and your warrant." *Papa's voice is strong. How can he sound so calm?*

"Eh-en, so! You think say I dey play? Open am now, now!"

"I am not playing either. I follow the rules. Pass your warrant through here first. If it's in order I shall of course open up."

Sade is squeezing Mama's hand.

Femi is crying. "Why have they come, Mama? What are they going to do to Papa?"

What would the police do to them? The unspoken question whipped through Sade's brain as they huddled in the corner close to the shattered glass. Video Man had shut his ears to their pleas to let them go. Huffing and puffing, he stalked back and forth from his counter across the littered floor to the locked door. He cursed hooligans and he cursed the police for taking so long.

A flickering blue light and a siren announced the arrival of the police. Video Man's hand trembled as he jostled with the key. Two police officers, a man and a woman, stepped calmly inside and glanced around the shop. The man looked especially tall with his high black helmet next to the woman with her pot-shaped hat. As Video Man spoke in a furious stream, both officers listened with folded arms. The policeman's gaze shifted so silently and coolly that, before she could look away, Sade found herself caught for a moment. Video Man broke off.

"Well, what are you going to do?" he demanded.

"Can you tell us again, sir—what exactly did you see these kids do?" asked Cool Gaze.

"I've just told you!" Tiny bubbles of froth appeared at the edge of Video Man's lips. "The others sent 'em in to distract me. You could tell from the way they looked at each other! And three of 'em was black as these two."

"But what did you actually see them do? Did either of

these two kids do any of this?" Cool Gaze pointed to the mess strewn around the floor and the shattered window.

The woman officer took the children aside. She pulled a notepad and pencil out of her pocket.

"I need to know your names, your parents' names and where you live. I'll start with you." Miss Police Business raised her eyebrows at Sade. The pencil remained poised above the pad.

"Do you understand me?" Miss Police Business spoke a little louder and slower. "You have to tell me your names."

Sade stared at the notepad. Miss Police Business turned to Femi.

"Well, let me ask you then. What is your name?"

Femi's eyes remained glued on his sneakers.

"Well, who are your parents? What are their names?" The voice was sharper now.

Sade felt as if her brain had crashed. Like Papa's computer. When that happened, you could tap in as many commands as you liked but nothing would come out.

"Do we know if they speak English?" asked Cool Gaze.

"Oh they speak English all right. I heard 'em!" declared Video Man.

Cool Gaze now towered them.

"Look. If you've done nothing wrong, there's no need to be frightened."

Papa has read the piece of paper and Joseph opens the gate. Men in khaki uniform and black berets surge into the yard. Papa is surrounded. Mama lets out a small cry.

"Stay here!" she orders the children and rushes out of the sitting room to get to the yard. By the time she sprints down the steps, the police have hustled Papa out of the gates.

"Where are you taking him?" Mama cries.

Sade glimpses Papa's white shirt among the khaki as police push him into the back of their truck. No one answers Mama. The children run outside. When they reach Mama, the truck is already roaring down the road.

Sade had never felt so cold in all her life. Frozen inside and out. None of the people standing in front of her and Femi made any sense. The crazed Video Man still frothing at the side of his whitened mouth like their neighbor's old guard-dog. Miss Police Business with an irritated frown like Sade's teacher, Miss Okoya, when a student had disobeyed her. Cool Gaze with his searching green eyes as pale as unripe almonds.

The police officers moved to the counter. They talked in low voices before coming back. Miss Police Business spoke briskly.

"If you refuse to tell us who you are and where you live, we shall have to take you to a place of safety."

"What? Aren't you going to arrest 'em?" butted in Video Man. "Make 'em tell you about their friends?"

"Not enough evidence for that, sir," said Cool Gaze.

"Useless lot!" Video Man muttered loudly, turning his back.

"Come on, you two!" Miss Police Business pointed to the door. "You're coming with us to the police station. The Emergency—"

Sade's mind crashed again.

CHAPTER 12

STATE OF EMERGENCY

THE PHOTOGRAPHS ARE SPREAD across Papa's desk. He has brought them home to show Mama after returning late at night. They don't notice Sade creeping into the study. Silent tears slip down Mama's cheeks.

"How can they do this, Folarin? Wasting such young lives!"

Mama holds up a picture. Bodies sprawled over the grass. She picks up another. A young man's body slumped across steps, arms clawing forward. As if he was trying to get up the stairs but didn't make it.

"Where was this, Folarin? Where was he?"

"Outside the library."

Mama shakes her head, almost in disbelief.

It was the same university where Papa and Mama had met as students. Papa had traveled up there to report on "student disturbances," as the authorities called them. The students had planned a large demonstration that started off loud and noisy but not violent. They intended marching into town with their placards. GENERALS CLEAR OUT! FREE ELECTIONS! NIGERIA WANTS A FREE PRESS! RELEASE ALL POLITICAL PRISONERS! But before they had even left the campus, a convoy of army trucks had arrived, crammed with soldiers. They spread from the trucks like flies. The shooting began without warning.

Sade remains very still, listening to Papa tell Mama what he has seen. He is hardly at home these days. There are so many terrible reports about what the soldiers are doing. Some newspapers are too scared to publish them. Others have been shut down, but Papa's newspaper has been moving from office to office to stop the soldiers' finding them. Papa says the Brass Buttons like to pretend to the world and themselves that everything is normal. But actually they are living under a state of emergency.

Two days later, after the photos and story were published, the soldiers came to take Papa away.

CHAPTER 13

TWO PARCELS, NO ADDRESS

A YOUNG MAN, WITH GINGER HAIR hanging in a tail behind his neck, examined them from across the bare wooden table. His face was serious but not unfriendly. Miss Police Business had brought him into the room where they had been waiting nervously.

"This is the Emergency Social Worker," she began.

"Hello. I am Robert." He bowed his head slightly forward in a greeting.

"I'd like you to come with me. I think you need somewhere safe to stay for the night," he continued in a soft, unhurried voice. "I shall try and find something for you. Is that OK?"

Sade looked at Femi. Neither had spoken from the time the police arrived at the video shop. Since their journey in the police car, Femi's body had become almost rigid. His eyes avoided his sister but Sade knew he would follow whatever she did. She tapped his hand lightly as she stood up and, without a word, walked in silence to the door.

Sade didn't even try to take in where they were going as they were driven away. Outside everything was strange and threatening. Darth Vaders in alleys. Thieves. Vandals. Crazed people. Police who might lock you up because you couldn't tell them who you were or who your parents were or where you lived. Sade knew they would certainly be asked the same questions again. At the moment she and Femi were like two parcels with no address. They could end up anywhere.

The car pulled up at a low building squashed between two gloomy blocks of flats. Most of the building was in darkness but there were lights in the entrance and inside a couple of windows. The children trailed behind Robert with the hair-tail along empty corridors to an office. Inside was a desk scattered with papers next to a computer, some comfortable chairs and a box of toys in one corner. He pointed to the chairs and asked if they would like a hot drink. Sade and Femi each gave a small nod and he didn't press them to speak.

Left on their own, they could hear bits of his conversation on the telephone next door. Sade picked out the opening phrase "We're looking for a temporary foster home . . ." She lost track after the first few calls. Femi was half-asleep already, curled up over the rucksack on his knees. After sipping her hot chocolate, Sade closed her eyes.

The next she knew was that she was being gently shaken. Robert Hair-tail was telling them something about a lady who was willing to take them in for a night or two.

"It's only temporary. Mrs. Graham has a boy of her own and takes care of twins. I'm afraid you'll have to share their bedrooms. Not ideal. But I know you'll be safe and warm with Mrs. Graham while we explore how best to help you. OK? Are you ready to come?"

Sade had to make a real effort to pull herself out of the chair. If only they could have been just left to sleep where they were in this office with hot chocolate, toys and scattered papers. It was going to be much more scary to be taken into some strange person's home. Worse still to share some unknown person's bedroom. She was sure Femi was thinking the same thing. His head was completely bowed as he hauled himself up. Getting up looked even more painful for him than old Baba Akin at Family House shifting his ancient bones.

"I know it's difficult but you'll be fine with Mrs. Graham."

Robert Hair-tail seemed concerned to reassure them. Mutely they followed him back out of the building.

Once again the car became a capsule traveling to some unknown destination. It turned out to be a massive block of flats along an almost deserted road. The dull glow from street-lamps and the ceiling lights above narrow open passageways cast eerie shadows. The lift was out of order and they had to walk up some poorly lit stairs. An awful smell of stale urine slunk in the corners.

"Be careful where you step. Sometimes there's glass," Robert warned them.

Sade felt Femi pitch a little closer to her. In Lagos there were flats that looked stained and dirty like this but they had never been inside them. All their relatives and friends lived in houses. Mostly houses and spacious compounds with yards and lawns, trees, flowers and fruits. She did not remember ever discussing who lived in the crowded stained-looking flats with Papa or Mama. She just assumed that they must be very poor people. What kind of place was this where Robert Hair-tail was bringing them?

On the fifth floor he branched off down the passage and knocked softly at number 59. A short, plump white woman opened the door. Her mouse-colored hair was drawn back from her face by a pink band.

"This is Mrs. Graham," said Robert.

"Come in quick. It's freezing out there!" said Mrs. Graham, greeting them.

As Sade stepped into a small room with a table on one side and sofa and chairs on the other, her first thought was that it looked clean and not at all dirty like the stairs. At least that was a relief.

"Robert says they don't know your names," continued Mrs. Graham. "What am I going to call you then?"

Sade and Femi remained silent.

"Aahh, well there's always tomorrow. You can tell us then. When you've had a bit of a rest, eh?"

"They're tired all right," said Robert. "We'll leave all the talking until the morning. One of the Children's Team will come over."

"Looks like they've been places! Know what I mean? I'll show them their beds straight away. Kevin!"

A boy about Sade's age dragged himself off the leatherlike sofa in front of the television. Sighing loudly, he ambled over to them.

"This is my son, Kevin."

Sade's eyes flicked between the smiling mother and the unsmiling boy. There was a strong likeness between the two of them. The boy shared his mother's plump cheeks and narrow forehead but not her pale complexion and green eyes. His skin was distinctly light brown and his hair dark, short and curly. For a fleeting moment Sade wondered about Mr. Graham but Robert Hair-tail had made no mention of him.

"Take this young man to your room, Kevin. Give him the bottom bed and you move up top. Mind you show him the bathroom on the way."

Protest was written all over Kevin's face.

"Aw, Mum! You always give me grief! Why can't he sleep with the twins?"

"I've told you already. The girl is going to sleep with the twins. There's not even room to swing a cat in there. Now get moving!"

Kevin kissed his teeth and muttered something under his breath. Sade saw Femi's jaw set. She half expected him to refuse to go. To do his "I'm staying here until I'm satisfied" act. But Femi was so tired that when Kevin brushed past him, he tramped behind without a word.

Ten minutes later when Mrs. Graham showed her to a camp bed, Sade hardly noticed the small shapes on the other two beds, fitted at right angles to each other. Mrs. Graham handed her an oversize T-shirt.

"Sleep tight!" she said. "This'll do as a nightie if you need one."

Sade suddenly felt so limp that it took all her energy just to tug off her shoes, climb into the bed and pull the quilt over her. Mrs. Graham's T-shirt slid off the bed onto the floor.

CHAPTER 14

VOICES IN THE DARK

SADE IS TRYING TO PACK books into her schoolbag. She is struggling to push them in but something is blocking them. She must hurry up. Papa has already called her twice. She's holding him up. Making him late. Why won't the books just slip in? She has to pull out the books that are already inside the bag and start packing it all over again.

Sade is slipping her English book into her schoolbag when she hears Mama scream. Two sharp cracks splinter the air. She hears her father's fierce cry, rising, falling.

"No! No!"

The revving of a car and skidding of tires smother his voice.

Her bag topples from the bed, spilling books, pen and pencil onto the floor. She races to the verandah, pushing past Femi in the doorway. His body is wooden with fright.

"Mama mi?" she whispers.

Papa is kneeling in the driveway, Mama partly curled up against him. One bare leg stretches out in front of her. His strong hands grip her, trying to halt the growing dark red monster. But it has already spread down her bright white uniform. It stains the earth around them.

• • •

Sade woke shaking and trembling to the sounds of crying and sobbing. She struggled to raise herself up on her elbow. Two small shapes squirmed and twisted on the beds next to her, one sitting upright and the other lying down. The camp bed squeaked as the upright child howled even more loudly. Sade's own cheeks were wet. Had she cried out in her sleep and woken the infants?

"Sshhh! Sshhh! Sorry!" Sade whispered. But hearing footsteps, she flung herself down and curled quickly back under the quilt, making a roof over her head. The door opened and Mrs. Graham came in, softly clucking.

"Aahhh, what's the matter then? Did you have a bad dream, Lizzie-girl? What's wrong, Johnny? It's only a friend come to sleep with you."

Sade heard Mrs. Graham shuffling through the narrow gap between the beds to reach the twins. Sade pressed her palm against her mouth to hold back her own weeping.

CHAPTER 15

TROUBLE WITH THE TRUTH

BLACK-AND-WHITE MICKEYS AND MINNIES were dancing in rows down the faded blue curtains when Sade woke. A dull light filtered through the material between the dancing figures. For a few seconds she was confused. Where were her bright-yellow sunflower curtains and the golden streaks of light calling her to join the day? Instead chilly air tingled her nose and face.

The room was very still. Sade rolled over, making the camp bed squeak. Quilts matching the Mickey and Minnie curtains lay rumpled on the other two beds. Mrs. Graham must have taken the infants out. In the middle of the night? Or this morning before she was awake? All she could remember was Mrs. Graham trying to calm their wild crying with soothing words. Hidden under the bedcovers, she had ached for Mama's arms. After that she knew nothing until waking again now.

She studied Minnie with her red ribbon and smiling Mickey with his blue bow tie. There would be more questions today. What are your names, where are your parents, where do you live, what are you doing here, how did you get here, have you got any relatives? And so on and on . . . She needed to sort out her own thoughts first. Yesterday they had behaved like crazed butterflies trapped under a jar. If Papa could have seen them like that, he would have pressed his face against the jar urging them to stop.

Slow down! Think! Remember the children who entered the forest all on their own? When they met the small drum and heard it thumping, they should have stopped. Instead they jumped over it and traveled in deeper. The medium-sized drum tried to warn them too but they just raced around it and got even more lost. So it was too late by the time they stumbled into the largest drum . . . the swallowing drum! It gulped them down. And that would have been that except, luckily for them, their mother came to rescue them.

But your mother can't.

Right now, Papa couldn't rescue them either and they had no idea how long it would take him to arrive. So what should they say when the questions started again? Mama always said, *Truth keeps the hand cleaner than soap.*

Yet look what trouble had come through Papa writing the truth in his newspaper.

Every now and again, Sade heard walking or running footsteps outside the window. It sounded as if the bedroom was next to the passageway. She buried her head in the pillow. Who would come to question them? Miss Police Business or Cool Gaze? She winced at the thought. Or the Emergency man with the ginger hair-tail, what was his name . . . Robert?

But it was someone else who sat on Mrs. Graham's sofa later that morning studying them. Mrs. Graham had insisted that they borrow her son's tracksuits so they wouldn't catch colds. Kevin had already left for school and they were not looking forward to his return. It was bad enough having to wear a stranger's clothes without that person giving you nasty looks.

The lady on the sofa smiled at the children. Her eyebrows arched like a bird in flight and Sade was immediately reminded of her own Iyawo. Here was the same steady gaze as from the figure on her desk! If Iyawo came alive and her ebony plaits could hang down instead of rising into a crown this was surely how she would look with her wood transformed into soft rich brown skin. However, when the lady spoke, it was not with a Nigerian accent. She sounded more like a newsreader from the little radio on the sideboard, on Papa's beloved BBC World Service.

Iyawo's twin introduced herself as Jenny from the Children's Team. She was a social worker with Robert who had already told her how the children had been found. She and Robert wanted to help, she said, but could only do so if they knew more about them. She would like to start by knowing their names.

Sade's heart pounded. This Iyawo-Jenny sounded friendly, yet how could they be sure? It was the police who had handed them over to Robert Hair-tail, so anything they said to this lady might go back to the police. What if the police in England sent the information to the police in Nigeria? Then they would know that Folarin Solaja's children had escaped to England and the Brass Button officers at the airport would be on alert for Papa himself.

Iyawo-Jenny tried again.

"You do speak English, don't you?"

She asked the question so gently that it seemed terribly rude not to reply. Sade gave a very slight nod.

"Good. Robert said he thought you understood him. There's no need to be frightened because we only want to help you," Iyawo-Jenny reassured. "Have you run away from home?"

Both children kept their heads lowered.

"Look, if you've run away, and think your parents will be angry, then we shall try to help you sort things out."

The more the social worker spoke, the more Sade's mind spun. Femi's feet nervously tapped the carpet. They couldn't keep silent forever, thought Sade. They needed help to find Uncle Dele. But what could they say that was safe?

"Would you rather write your names for me?" asked Iyawo-Jenny, offering her pad and a pencil. Reluctantly Sade placed the pad on her lap. She hesitated, looking to Femi for a response. But Femi had kept his eyes averted from her and everyone else all morning. He seemed to be sunk into the oversize tracksuit and himself. Surely they could not avoid giving their names? Sooner or later they would be forced to say them and Iyawo-Jenny certainly seemed less frightening than Miss Police Business or Cool Gaze. Aware of the social worker's eyes on her, Sade carefully printed SADE and FEMI.

Iyawo-Jenny stretched over to read.

"What lovely names," she said. "Can you write your surname too?"

Head still down and the blood rushing to her cheeks,
Sade printed ADEWALE. Femi's feet stopped jiggling. It was
their mother's family name.

"Where do you live?" asked Iyawo-Jenny softly.

Slowly Sade printed IBADAN. The city close to their
home village. She prayed that Femi wouldn't say anything. It
wasn't a complete lie. They often spent time with Grandma
there in the holidays. But it wasn't really the truth.

"That's in Nigeria, isn't it?" said Iyawo-Jenny. "Is that
where you've come from?"

Sade gave a tiny nod.

"Ahh! That's interesting. When did you arrive?" asked
Iyawo-Jenny quietly.

Sade did not reply. Iyawo-Jenny changed the question.

"Did you arrive yesterday?"

Another small nod.

"Did you come by yourselves?"

Sade shook her head.

"Did you come with your parents—and somehow get
lost?"

Femi stiffened beside her, pushing his feet against the
carpet. Before Sade was able to wipe it away, a large tear
dropped on to the pad on her lap.

CHAPTER 16

REFUGEES?

IYAWO-JENNY PUT HER ARM gently around Sade's shoulder, trying to comfort her. Femi shifted out of reach, farther along the sofa. Iyawo-Jenny tried a few more yes/no questions, which Sade answered in small nods and shakes. But the social worker did not learn much more. Only that the children had come without their parents and that something unexpected had happened in Nigeria. Something dangerous enough for the children to be sent to London. But she learned nothing about what had actually happened to Mama and Papa. And also nothing about Mrs. Bankole or Uncle Dele.

"It sounds as if we shall have to apply for asylum for you," Iyawo-Jenny said finally. "That means asking if you can stay here for reasons of safety. You know, to be treated as refugees. Nigeria has been in the news a lot because of what happened to Ken Saro-Wiwa."

The surprise must have shown in Sade's face. Mr. Saro-Wiwa had been at university with Uncle Tunde in Ibadan. Papa had been writing about him and the other Ogoni leaders locked up in jail. Papa's newspaper had been protesting for months that the Brass Buttons weren't going to give them a fair trial.

"Aahh, that poor man! Terrible what they did to him, wasn't it?" Mrs. Graham had come in from the kitchen. "So are these two from that same country, all the way from Africa then? And there's me thinking you'd just had a little spot of bother at home down the road!"

Iyawo-Jenny's midnight-calm eyes were solemn as she turned to the children. "Try not to worry too much. Whatever it was, you have obviously had a frightening experience. You can tell us more when you're feeling a little better."

She explained that Mrs. Graham would take them to buy some winter clothes and that they would stay with her for a few days until other arrangements could be made. If possible, Iyawo-Jenny said she wanted to find a Nigerian family to take care of them.

Sade returned to the bedroom. She curled up on the camp bed under the quilt to think about what Iyawo-Jenny had said. Refugees? They were those winding lines of starving people, with stick-thin children. People who carried their few possessions in dusty cotton bundles, struggling across deserts and mountains. Refugees were people trying to escape famine and war. You saw them on television. Were she and Femi really refugees? She wondered if she had done the right thing, not giving their true surname. It was so difficult to know what was right and wrong anymore. And doing the right thing could lead to awful things happening. Mama knew that. She had tried to warn Papa. They had heard the shocking news about Mr. Saro-Wiwa on Papa's World Service, sitting together at the dining table.

"*It has been confirmed that this morning the Nigerian*

authorities executed the political activist and writer Ken Saro-Wiwa and eight other Ogonis . . ."

Papa's head is bowed in his hands. Mama prays. Sade and Femi join her. Even Papa joins in the "Amen." Afterward Mama implores in her tender way.

"Please, Folarin, please take care. If they can do this to Ken, they will do anything. These people don't care even what the whole world thinks."

"I shall be careful, don't worry." Papa's face is somber. "But I have to be able to face myself in the mirror. And our children need to know that bad men succeed when the rest of us look the other away."

Papa had spent the whole weekend working furiously on an article about the executions. That's why he had been eager to get to the office early that morning. On the day the gunmen came . . .

Mrs. Graham put her head around the door. Her next-door neighbor had a daughter Sade's age and might be able to lend Sade a few warm clothes. Did Sade want to come with her? When Sade shook her head, Mrs. Graham didn't try to force her.

"Will you be all right on your own? I'm only next door. Expect you just want to get used to things, don't you? Jenny says she'll sort out the money and we'll go and buy some new clothes tomorrow, yeah?"

After she heard the front door close, Sade slipped back to Femi in front of the television. Single-handed, Superman was knocking out a bunch of mean-looking guards. The people who had been rescued were gasping, then smiling with relief. There was a lot of shaking hands and congratulations before Superman flew up and away into the sky. The program that followed was much less exciting. Four people sitting behind a long table, talking.

"Too boring!" said Femi, turning off the button.

Sade wanted to talk.

"Femi, was it all right, giving Mama's name—to the lady this morning?" Sade was anxious to know what he thought. Ignoring the question, Femi wandered over to the sideboard. Sade followed.

A telephone and a thick directory lay beside a silver-framed photograph of a little boy with a maroon bow tie, dark twinkling eyes and a head full of black curls. It looked like Kevin when he was younger. Another photograph showed him in the same outfit laughing as he sat on Mrs. Graham's lap. There was no picture of Mr. Graham. Femi began flicking through the pages of the book.

"See if Uncle Dele is there!" Sade felt a wave of hope. Of course, why hadn't they thought of looking in a directory yesterday? The excitement didn't last long. There was not a single Solaja.

Femi went on browsing.

"Look! Nigeria!" Femi had found a list of codes for different countries with names of towns and cities. Abeokuta . . . Ibadan . . . Kano . . . Lagos.

Femi picked up the handset of the telephone.

"Let's try to ring, Sade—I want to talk to Papa!" he pleaded.

"It costs a lot. We must ask first."

"I just want to hear what the ringing sounds like from here. I'll put it down straight away, I promise!"

As Femi dialed, Sade's eyes switched nervously back and forth to the front door. What if Mrs. Graham came back right away and found them? Femi tapped the final digit. There was silence, then some clicks and silence again. Femi sucked in his breath. He was not going to give up. Checking the code, he dialed again. Once more there was silence then clicks. But this time they were followed by a high-pitched hum. Whatever it was, it wasn't a telephone ringing.

In the evening, when Kevin was sprawled out on the sofa and the twins already in bed, Sade went to Mrs. Graham in the kitchen. She had been answering Mrs. Graham's questions with nods and shakes of her head. Now she would have to talk.

"Can you help us make a call to our uncle in Nigeria please?" The question came out as a whisper. Mrs. Graham stopped wiping the table and asked Sade to repeat it. Femi hung by the doorway, watching. They had decided it was best not to mention Papa.

"Ooh dear, that's going to be a bit expensive! D'you know what I'm saying?" said Mrs. Graham when she had understood. "Perhaps the social workers can do it for you at their office? Yeah, why don't we ask them tomorrow?"

Sade was silent. They needed to speak to Papa now, not tomorrow. Her eyes misted over and Mrs. Graham put down her cloth.

"All right, all right!" she reassured the children. "We don't want tears. Let's make the call and I'll sort out the money with Jenny later."

"Yeah, that's typical, Mum!" Kevin had come up behind Femi. "You don't even let me chat with my mates, going on about your phone bill."

"Don't be cheeky, young man! You see your friends every day at school. So don't go comparing yourself with Sade and Femi." Mrs. Graham looked at him sharply.

"Oh yeah, yeah, yeah!" Kevin crooned, ambling back to the sofa.

Sade jotted down their home number on the telephone pad while Mrs. Graham got lost in the directory searching for the code to Nigeria. The children had to bite their lips not to tell her where to find it. Sade explained that their uncle lived in Lagos. She was sure that Mrs. Graham would pass on the information to Iyawo-Jenny. When Mrs. Graham finally dialed, Sade willed the clicks to end, to switch to the ringing tone. Would Papa still be at home, she wondered? Or had Uncle Tunde persuaded him to go somewhere safer? If Papa wasn't there, Joseph would be. They never left the house completely empty. Joseph always looked after it for them. She could already imagine the surprise and delight in his voice at hearing them speak all the way from London. Whoever answered, she would talk in Yoruba, so Mrs. Graham would not understand.

But the clicks were followed by silence. Mrs. Graham tried twice more. It was the same every time.

"Do you have trouble with your phones in Nigeria then?"

she asked. Sade didn't know what to say. "Well, well! This is turning into quite a palaver, d'you know what I mean? I'll get the operator to check it for us." Mrs. Graham sighed.

The operator called back thirty minutes later. He had spoken to someone at the telephone exchange in Nigeria who had checked the number. The report was that the line had been cut off. It was completely dead.

CHAPTER 17

LIES THICKEN

THE ELEGANT LADY AT THE DOOR reminded Sade so strongly of Mama Buki that she was taken aback. It was something in the lady's assured, confident face. Her black and green *gele* was also wrapped above her broad forehead in Mama Buki's favorite style, the corners of the headscarf perched up like the tails of two little birds. Iyawo-Jenny stood beside her, smiling.

"Mrs. Appiah is from Ghana. She works for the Refugee Council here. She's an adviser for refugee children and I've brought her to meet you and Femi."

"Thank y—," Sade dropped her voice to a mumble. She suddenly realized that she didn't know what to call Iyawo-Jenny. Yesterday the social worker had introduced herself simply as Jenny. Back at home, for children to call her by her first name would be rude.

"May we come in?" asked Iyawo-Jenny.

Sade pressed backward against the door, embarrassed.

Mrs. Appiah talked with the children as if she had always known them but simply hadn't seen them for a while. She asked about school, their teachers and friends and their favorite games. She spoke in a way that made it almost seem that everything was normal. Like Iyawo-Jenny, she began with questions that could be answered without speaking. She had a way of probing and smiling just like Mama Buki, too. In between her questions, she told them about her own days at school, stories about friends and rivals, fearsome teachers and getting into trouble. Slowly she coaxed Sade into single words, then into short sentences. Even Femi was drawn into listening and finally into whispering the number of goals he had scored for his school football team last term.

Iyawo-Jenny slipped away, leaving the three of them alone on the sofa.

"Tell me now—how are things there at home?" Mrs. Appiah asked gently.

Sade winced and shut her eyes. It was as if another blanket had been thrown over her, smothering her voice and everything else. She felt Mrs. Appiah taking her hand. Sade wanted to pull it back but the strong warm grip held it firmly yet without squeezing.

"I can tell that something terrible has happened—it's hard for you to speak about it—but it's very important—so we can help you . . . and call me Auntie or Mama, like children back there, at your home."

Softly and surely, the words threaded through Sade's darkness. An arm enclosed her.

She is silently wrapped in Mama Buki's arms. Mama Buki is reaching out to pull Femi in. Sade feels him soften as their aunt presses them close. They are enclosed in the heat of the day and the warmth of Mama Buki's body. But the sound of

*weeping winds its way through the house, seeking her out,
seeping into her.*

Great sobs stirred inside Sade like gusts of wind whipping up
palm leaves before a storm.

"We all need to cry sometimes," Mama Appiah consoled
quietly. "Cry and let it out."

Sade gave up trying to hold back her tears.

She wasn't sure for how long she cried, but slowly, as her
crying began to subside, she became aware of how comforting Mama Appiah's arm felt. She glanced at Femi. He was
silent and dry-eyed but with a look of such sadness that Sade's
tears threatened to swell up again.

"When you are ready, I want you both to help me understand your story," said Mama Appiah. The birds' tails
swooped gently with her *gele* as she turned to each of them.

"Take all the time you need."

For a while Sade sat tongue-tied. Conflicting thoughts
raced through her brain. Part of her wanted to tell Mama
Appiah the whole truth, including that she had given Iyawo-
Jenny a false surname. But fear stopped her. When Papa was
safely in England, then it would be different. They wouldn't
need to worry anymore about police and soldiers at home
because Papa would be with them. Until then, it was better
that they were Sade and Femi Adewale. Was it safe, at least,
to tell Mama Appiah about Uncle Dele? If they didn't find
him, how would Papa ever know where to look for them when
he got to London? Perhaps Mama Appiah could help them. It
was a risk they would have to take.

"Our uncle . . . he's in London," Sade began, "but . . . but we don't know where he is."

Stumbling a little at first, she told how they had gone to the College of Art only to find that Uncle Dele was missing. She gave his name, Dr. Solaja, but let Mama Appiah think that he was Mama's brother. When Mama Appiah asked how they had entered the country, Sade simply replied that they had come with "a lady." Mama Appiah didn't press any further.

Three days later, Mama Appiah escorted the children by bus from Mrs. Graham's flat to the office of Mr. Nathan, a refugee lawyer. Sade flicked over the pages of a magazine in the small waiting room, trying to hide her nervousness. If this Mr. Nathan was anything like Uncle Tunde, they could be in trouble. Papa used to joke that Uncle Tunde should have been a detective rather than a lawyer because he was so good at getting to the truth.

"Of course lawyers have to be good detectives! And if they are anything like your Uncle Tunde, they are also brain surgeons—looking inside their clients' heads!"

Did that mean this Mr. Nathan would know when they weren't telling the truth? Sade had tried to talk with Femi about what they should say, but he refused to show any interest. All he seemed to do was watch television and play on his own with the twins' Legos. For the last few days, he had hardly even spoken to her.

The man who came out to shake hands with Mama Appiah limped across the room, one foot sweeping the carpet.

He was short with a small wind-beaten face that made Sade think of an old sailor rather than a lawyer. A tuft of graying hair hung over his forehead down to his spectacles like a clutch of dried grass. He greeted Mama Appiah like an old friend before turning to the children and inviting them to follow him into his office. When he smiled, his gray-green eyes seemed to ripple and light up his face.

Leaning across a wooden desk that looked even more worn than himself, Mr. Nathan began by explaining what they would have to do to get permission to stay in England. Sade soon lost track. Asylum, immigration officers, forms, questionnaires, interviews . . . it all sounded strange and difficult. The desk was as untidy as Papa's, scattered with papers. A forest of books surrounded them, stretching from the floor to the ceiling, while files stacked on the carpet rose up like a thick undergrowth. But instead of the scented pink magnolias outside the window of Papa's study, the rain-stained glass revealed a dense cluster of dull brick and concrete buildings under a drab sky.

It was only a short interview. Mama Appiah briefly told Mr. Nathan what Sade had already told her, including the information about Uncle Dele. She had already made enquiries at the Art College herself and there was no further news of him. Mr. Nathan wrote down the children's full names with Sade spelling out Folasade and Olufemi Adewale. Sade was relieved that Femi let her speak for him. In his don't-care mood he might easily give away their real names. Mr. Nathan also asked for their dates and place of birth.

"So you are Nigerian," he said. "And is that where you have come from? Nigeria?"

Sade nodded.

"Well that's all we need at this stage to get you Temporary Admission. But later you will have to explain more about why your family thought you were in danger—and why they sent you here without proper passports. The immigration officers will also want to know how you came into the country."

Although Mr. Nathan spoke without any threat in his voice, his words triggered something in Femi, setting him off like a firecracker.

"We came with a lady but we don't know her name!" he blurted.

Sade stared at her brother.

"Did the lady tell you her name but you have forgotten it?" asked Mr. Nathan. He scanned both children as Mrs. Bankole's words rang in Sade's ears.

"If you tell anyone my name, my friend in Lagos will never help your father."

Sade hesitated. Keeping quiet was easier than lying.

"She didn't tell us," Femi mumbled.

"I'm sorry. I didn't hear that," said Mr. Nathan.

"Didn't tell us," Femi repeated more loudly. He kept his eyes fixed on his new sneakers, which were busy scuffing the carpet.

"You know it will be very important that you tell us everything but this will do for now." Mr. Nathan spoke patiently. Sade felt her cheeks were burning. Surely even Mama would have understood why they dare not tell the whole truth?

CHAPTER 18

HAWK LADY AND HAWK MAN

THEIR FIRST MEETING WITH MR. NATHAN had taken less than an hour, but their visit to the Immigration Office took the whole day. Sade had overheard the lawyer say to Mama Appiah that he would come with them himself, in case there was trouble. Waiting at London Bridge Station for Mr. Nathan to join them, the children had their photographs taken inside a small self-service booth. Mama Appiah explained that they would need them for their forms. The two strips of faces that were finally tossed out looked nothing like the cheerful fair-haired boy and smiling lady pictured on the front of the booth.

The train journey took them overground across south London. There were stretches when they were high up and could see mile after mile of houses and buildings. Everything seemed to have absorbed the dreary grayness from the sky. Sade closed her eyes.

Standing on the steps of Grandma's church in Ibadan, near the top of the hill, you can also see for miles. Thousands upon thousands of rust-colored roofs, all the same dry red as the dust beneath your feet. Voices travel from the street below the church. A mingling of Yoruba, Queen's English, Pidgin English. Sounds as warm and rich as the sunshine colors worn by passersby.

The cold crept under Sade's navy-blue anorak as they trudged from the station a little behind Mr. Nathan. Despite his limp, he set a vigorous pace. They kept their heads down, trying to protect their faces from the wind. But as they emerged from a subway and craned their necks to look up at the immigration building, they couldn't avoid the freezing blast. The gray concrete and glass soared upward like a cannon aimed at the clouds. At the base of the building, a small throng of figures huddled between two rows of bars outside a large revolving door underneath the words IMMI-GRATION AND NATIONALITY DEPARTMENT. A man in a yellow coat guarded the door. With one hand, he held a mobile tele-phone up to his ear. With the other, he controlled the queue. He allowed one or two people to pass, then thrust out his arm like a barricade.

"We always have to wait, wait, wait." Mama Appiah sighed as they joined the end of the queue. "My grandmother said you can throw pebbles at an elephant and he'll still ignore you! I always feel like that here."

Wedging herself next to Mama Appiah, Sade watched Mr. Nathan approach Mr. Mobile. Mr. Mobile shook his head and Mr. Nathan frowned. When he joined them, he was still frowning.

"This place only gets worse! All this—twenty floors of office space—and not a decent waiting room!" He jerked his head upward. "It really is a disgrace! No other government department makes people wait outside like this!"

It really is a disgrace!

Sade could hear Papa saying the selfsame words. However, even inside her head, Papa sounded more explosive. Mr. Nathan must be trained in keeping cool like Uncle Tunde. But she could tell he was angry. They were lucky to have him on their side. But what would happen when he asked them to tell him everything? Would he not get angry with them when they still kept quiet?

Mr. Nathan's words to the guard seemed to have had some effect. The queue began to move a little more quickly until after quarter of an hour or so it was their turn to escape the biting wind and enter the building. Inside, it was like at the airport. Officers in black-and-white uniforms checked Mr. Nathan's briefcase and Mama Appiah's handbag before directing them through a metal-detector doorway. Uniformed officers stood at the base of the stairs and on the landings. They seemed to be everywhere. The children traipsed behind Mr. Nathan up a couple of flights and through a door marked ASYLUM SCREENING UNIT. There they joined another queue under the sign RECEPTION. Sade studied the long crowded room to her right. Most of the seats were occupied and the room hummed with a variety of voices, accents and languages. She tried to listen to those nearest to her but, apart from English, she didn't recognize any of the languages. Once again she was reminded of her encyclopedia and its picture of people from around the world. But the faces here looked much more tense and troubled than the people on the train to

Victoria Station. Were all these people trying to escape because of dangers in their own countries? A counter ran along the front length of the room. It was divided into small cubicles, each with a glass panel and a number. Although there was a whole line of cubicles, only four of them were in use. From time to time, a high-pitched buzzer would shriek, a number would light up in red on the board at the front, and another small group of people would make their way up to the immigration officer behind the glass.

From Reception, however, they were sent to the opposite side of the room. Here they joined the back row of a cluster of people sitting much more quietly than those on the right. Mr. Nathan explained that this was where they had to wait to be fingerprinted. Femi, who had been silent for most of the journey, now broke his silence.

"Do they think we are thieves?" he muttered fiercely.

"Many people say that children should not be finger-printed," said Mr. Nathan quietly. "But I'm afraid the rules allow it."

A lady in a white coat and white vinyl gloves stood by a door calling some people in and letting others out. She was dressed like a nurse or a doctor but Sade had the feeling that she was not really a medical person. The way she inspected everyone reminded Sade of a hawk and made her feel even more nervous. When, at last, it was their turn to go into the fingerprint room, Femi refused to move.

"They won't give us our papers, Femi! We *have* to do it," Sade whispered. She was aware of people looking at them.

"Does he speak English?" Hawk Lady asked loudly. "Tell him it won't hurt."

"Mrs. Appiah and I will come in with you," said Mr. Nathan. "It won't take long."

Femi dragged himself from his chair, glaring at Hawk Lady. Inside the room, two more people in white coats and gloves were waiting. The man was pushing a roller back and forth on a large inkpad while the lady was preparing sheets of paper. Sade watched as their full names were carefully written out, each on to a separate sheet below a printed grid of ten blank squares. Mama Appiah and Mr. Nathan stood behind them, close enough for Sade to hear Mama Appiah sigh. Picking up Sade's left hand, Hawk Lady led her to the counter with the inkpad.

"This won't hurt." Her lips curved into a smile.

Hawk Lady pressed each of Sade's fingers first onto the pad and then on to an empty square on the paper. A pattern of twirls and hillocks filled up the row of squares. If she and Femi had just been experimenting, it could have been fun. But with Hawk Lady clutching her fingers in this awful place, the dark stains of purple on her fingertips made her feel dirty all over. Releasing her grip, Hawk Lady pointed to taps and a sink.

Hawk Man now began with Femi.

"You must relax," he ordered.

But Femi held his arm so stiffly that the man had to struggle to raise her brother's hand up to the pad.

"This isn't going to work unless you relax," he repeated. He appealed to Mama Appiah. "Can you tell him in his own language that I'm not going to hurt him?"

Mama Appiah moved quickly to put a hand on Femi's shoulder.

"He understands your English perfectly," she said calmly. "He is tense because he thinks that fingerprinting is what they do to criminals."

With a sharp tug, Femi pulled his hand away. He folded his arms tightly around him.

"This is ridiculous," declared Mr. Nathan, addressing Hawk Lady. "You are causing the child unnecessary distress. These children are in the care of Social Services and Mrs. Appiah from the Refugee Council is also working with them. They are not going to run away. I cannot see the point of putting him through this."

"We're following the regulations, sir. What other proof do you have of their identity?"

"It is only a week since they arrived and —"

"But you still have no other proof," Hawk Lady interrupted, stretching her neck as if to mark a victory. Obviously they would not force the boy to have his fingerprints taken, she continued, beginning to sound impatient. But without them he was unlikely to be given his Temporary Admission papers. He should decide quickly because he was now holding up the queue. Femi must have been following it all because suddenly he thrust up his arm toward the inkpad, allowing Hawk Man to take hold of his hand. The set of his jaw showed that his teeth were clenched. They remained clenched even when he was washing the ink off his fingers.

On the other side of the room, they had to wait yet again.

While Mama Appiah and Mr. Nathan spoke to some of the people around them, Sade began to play a little guessing game with herself. Which countries did all these people come from? Her only clues were clothes and faces, and those weren't very reliable. But she liked testing her memory. What different countries were there in Asia, in South America, in Europe? Then she tried to remember names from the map of Africa above Papa's desk. Cameroon and Chad were next to Nigeria, but what was to the east of Chad? Sudan, Somalia? She puzzled over a woman in a lime green robe with purple flowers, her head covered with a scarf and her arms cradling a baby. A tiny wrinkled hand escaped from the hibiscus pink blanket, its fingers curled like little tendrils. The mother's face reminded Sade of sunken dunes in the desert. She sat so still, staring almost blankly, while her baby's fingers explored the empty air. Where was the baby's father, she wondered? Sade wanted Femi to join her quiz. They used to make up quizzes for each other, especially on long journeys in the car. Because she was older and had learned more at school, Femi used to get his own back by asking questions about sport. Sometimes they used to work in teams, one with Mama and the other with Papa. But when Sade asked Femi to make up a quiz with her now while they waited, he shrugged her off irritably. Instead he buried himself in the comic that Mama Appiah had bought him. Couldn't she see that he was busy?

When their number was finally called, the interview took hardly any time. The man behind the glass did not wear a uniform and looked young enough to be a student. His cropped brown hair stuck up straight like a brush. He asked exactly the same questions that Mr. Nathan had already asked them and Mr. Nathan did most of the talking. When Brush Head asked about their parents and how they had entered the country, Mr. Nathan replied that the children were still very frightened. They had come by air to London with a lady and they needed time to tell their full story. Sade clasped her hands together below the counter as Brush Head studied her and Femi before beginning to write. There was a form for each of them with their photographs pasted on the right-hand side. From upside down, Sade read the words "TEMPORARY ADMISSION." The forms were passed under the glass for them to sign. It was only then that Sade saw that above "Family Name: ADEWALE," Brush Head had written in bold large letters "CLAIMS TO BE." Did that mean he didn't believe them?

"Well, we got what we needed in the end," Mr. Nathan commented as they entered the subway. "Now that this is sorted"—he held up the folded papers—"you can start school."

Femi, who was ahead of them, whirled around in his tracks. Sade's mind somersaulted. School? She had been at her own school—Presentation High—just over a week ago. Already it seemed in another lifetime. She had been so happy in her class with all her friends. Her teacher, Miss Okoya, was very strict but really liked her. She had never imagined going to another school. Both Mama and Mama Buki had been boarders there when they were young. Presentation High was the only high school to which she had ever wanted to go.

Now, overnight, all these people were forcing her to do all these things she didn't want to do, to go to places she didn't want to be. Suddenly she knew just how angry Femi felt.

"I don't want to go to school here," she wanted to cry out. "We won't be staying here forever! Papa only sent us here to be safe with Uncle Dele!"

But her voice remained trapped.

CHAPTER 19

WELCOME

ANOTHER SHOCK AWAITED THE CHILDREN when Mama Appiah took them back to the flat. The first face Sade saw behind Mrs. Graham was Kevin's. He grinned as soon as he saw them and it wasn't a friendly grin. The twins looked up, then continued playing with their Legos. Stepping into the room, Sade realized that Iyawo-Jenny was there too.

"I was hoping you'd be back before I left. How did it go?" she asked.

"Aahh! I can see you're all washed out! Kevin, go and put on the kettle, there's a good boy." Mrs. Graham put her arms around Sade and Femi.

"When are you going to tell them then?" Kevin almost crowed. He didn't move from where he was leaning on the television, leering at them.

"Don't you be so nosy, my boy! Go and do as I say!"

Kevin sloped away, his tongue click-clocking to sound like a horse trotting off.

Iyawo-Jenny led the children to the sofa.

"I came round to tell you that we've managed to find you another foster family." The words floated in Sade's head for a few seconds, not making sense. Why *another foster family*? They were just getting used to being with Mrs. Graham, even if Kevin didn't like them.

"You remember I explained that Mrs. Graham was only able to take you on a temporary basis? It was an emergency to start with and that's why Mrs. Graham helped us out."

"They've been lovely children, no trouble at all," said Mrs. Graham.

"Mum!" Kevin yelled from the kitchen. "Your kettle's boiled."

"I'm going to take you to Mr. and Mrs. King tomorrow. Their children are grown-up, so you'll each be able to have a room to yourselves." Iyawo-Jenny looked earnestly from Sade to Femi. "I'm sure you'll like them too."

"I will still come to see you there," Mama Appiah reassured. "So don't worry!"

The adults were all smiling. How could Mama Appiah say 'don't worry'? They were surrounded by strangers in a strange land in which Uncle Dele—the only person who really knew them—had disappeared.

"The Kings are from Jamaica and Mr. King is very interested in Nigeria. You'll get on well, I know," Iyawo-Jenny encouraged. "And now that your permission to stay has been sorted out for a while, Mrs. King will organize for you to go to school."

Sade said nothing. With everything sorted out, what was there to say? They were simply being parceled up again and sent on to another address.

• • •

Mr. and Mrs. King lived in a quiet road of redbrick houses with arched doorways and small front gardens behind hedges, not very far from Mrs. Graham's flat. As they stood next to Iyawo-Jenny, waiting for the door to open, Sade knew from Femi's drooping figure that he was as miserable as she was. But Mama would have expected more of her.

You must help your brother, Sade. Sorrow is like a precious treasure, shown only to friends.

Sade imagined a string pulling up her head like a puppet.

The lady who invited them in had an open, pleasant face. She seemed quite tall but that might have been because her thick gray hair, drawn back from her light brown forehead, was piled up high and tied with a twist. Her neat-fitting blue dress with small yellow flowers gave her a bright air.

"We've been expecting you, mi dear!" Mrs. King greeted Iyawo-Jenny, then turned to the children. "We're very pleased to welcome you!"

Her voice moved with a light lilt.

"Indeed we are!"

Another voice as deep as a bass drum came from the back room. A powerfully built man entered the hallway with his arm stretched out to shake their hands. His hair was mottled with gray. He looked older than Uncle Tunde, but he still moved with a youthful swing. His face was as rich an ebony as Papa's with a strong, direct gaze and an easy smile.

Mr. King led them into a small sitting room. There were books and newspapers everywhere, unlike at Mrs. Graham's. Mrs. King followed with a tray of glasses and a jug of orange juice.

"Well," she said, "we hope you children will feel at home with us. Please call me Aunt Gracie and this is Uncle Roy."

"Who can say? We might even be related!" The rhythm in Uncle Roy's words matched his wife's. It was his dream, he said, to go one day to West Africa.

"It's the home of our ancestors, you know," he told them. Since he had retired from the post office he had been reading a lot about the African continent.

"I'm sure you children will teach me a thing or two, nuh?" he said.

"Give them time to settle now, before you start badgering them with questions!" Aunt Gracie chided him.

They were to have a bedroom each, one next to the other and both overlooking the back garden. Mrs. King explained that they had been their children's rooms. They were grown-up now and both living away from London. Sade's eyes were drawn to a small desk placed underneath the window and a bookshelf on the wall above the bed. The walls were painted a light ochre, like ripe corn, and the curtains and bedcover were patterned with the yellows and greens of pineapples. Femi's room was an emerald sea-green. Perhaps the Kings were trying to recall some of the light and colors from tropical Jamaica.

Sade found a *Girls' Annual* on the bookshelf in her room and, even though it was ten years out of date, she spent most of the afternoon on the bed reading. Toward evening, familiar smells from the kitchen forced her to interrupt the adventures in an English boarding school. She stared at the creases in the printed pineapples all around her and ached for Mama's voice to call her to eat.

Aunt Gracie had made them a special meal. Chicken stew with fried yams, fried plantains and a spinach soup that she had learned from a Nigerian friend. Femi tucked in without comment but Sade felt awkward, not wanting to talk but not wanting to be rude. The Kings seemed to have understood that the children were still reluctant to speak and for most of the meal carried on their own conversation. But just as they were finishing the meal with tinned guavas and cream, Aunt Gracie spoke about registering the children in school the following day. Femi would probably be accepted in Greenslades Primary and Sade at Avon, a large secondary school. They would then have a couple of days to get ready before starting school after the weekend.

"If your schools in Nigeria are like those in Jamaica, you'll find them quite different here, you know," Aunt Gracie said, as if in preparation. "Discipline in Jamaica is very firm. Certainly in my day it was."

"Don't be frightening them, Gracie! Before they even step foot in the place!"

Sade looked from one to the other. It was a bit like when Papa and Mama disagreed, Papa's voice suddenly sparking like a match. With adults, the meaning was often in what they didn't say. What did Uncle Roy mean by 'frightening them'? School had never been frightening to her. In fact, she had always loved going. But that was there, at home, not here. She was not looking forward to tomorrow.

CHAPTER 20

SEA OF FACES

THE DEAD, FLAT LOOK IN FEMI'S EYES added to Sade's own worries as she and Aunt Gracie left him in the headmistress's office at Greenslades Primary School the following Monday morning. He was going to join a Year Five class and Mrs. King could collect him from the school gates at three-fifteen.

"Don't worry! I'm sure he'll settle in soon," the headmistress said with a brightness matching the sparkle in her earrings. "He'll be wanting to walk home by himself then."

Sade wondered how she could be so sure. And what did she mean by "home" anyway?

At breakfast, when Aunt Gracie had prepared a pack of sandwiches for each of them, Femi had not even responded when asked what filling he would like. He had spent the weekend mostly with his head in a comic or watching sports on television. He had refused to come when Aunt Gracie took Sade out on Saturday to buy her new school uniform, even though he needed sports clothes for school. Every day he seemed to be moving farther away from her. When Sade waved good-bye to him from the headmistress's door, his arms hung so listlessly at his sides that the red plastic lunch box looked as if it might slide out from his fingers at any moment. She was used to seeing her brother angry and upset, but this deadness alarmed her. She hardly took any notice of the chattering children who swarmed up the stairs as Aunt Gracie spearheaded a path through them, down to the entrance. Crossing the tarmac playground to the gate in the high wire fence, she turned and looked back up at the three stories of the heavy old redbrick building. The ground floor with its lower windows protected by thick long bars made her think of a prison. It struck Sade that the only green in Greenslades Primary was in its name and the children's paintings on the walls inside.

Avon School was not far from Greenslades. Much newer, with ginger bricks, concrete and large plate-glass windows, it was set back from the road, also behind a high wire fence. Tall spiked gates opened on to a tarmac drive, lined on one side with a row of skeleton trees. Bushes bordering the dingy grass opposite looked as if they were chosen for their toughness. A few empty crisp packets on the drive and the grass provided the only patches of color.

Three days earlier, when they had come to register, the headmaster had immediately passed them on to his deputy, who in turn passed Sade on to be interviewed by a young woman teacher, Miss Harcourt. The teacher's name had struck her because it was the same as a city in Nigeria. She was wearing chocolate brown trousers and a pretty white blouse. No lady teacher at Presentation High ever wore trousers. Her long chestnut brown hair parted as smoothly as grain whenever she pushed it back through her fingers. She had invited Aunt

Gracie and Femi to accompany Sade into the interview room and began a string of questions. What languages did Sade speak? What was her old school, what class was she in, what subjects had she studied? Sade had answered with as few words as possible. But when Miss Harcourt stepped across the invisible line by asking with whom they had come to England, Sade had clammed up. Miss Harcourt's cheeks had flushed a deep crimson when Aunt Gracie mentioned refugees. Apologizing, the teacher had ended the interview by saying that she would place Sade with Year Eight. From the little that she had heard, added Miss Harcourt, Sade's English was good. The last remark had suprised Sade. Why shouldn't her English be good? Ever since she had learned to talk, she had been speaking English as well as Yoruba! There was even a family story that when she was very little, she would start a sentence in one language and end in the other. Papa used to joke that it meant she would always take the best of both worlds.

On the day of the interview, the other students had been in class. But now as they walked up the drive and into the entrance hall, Sade and Aunt Gracie were caught among the throng of boys and girls. Sade clutched her rucksack, feeling small and frightened as they wove their way through to the office. The lady at the office window pointed to chairs on the other side of the entrance hall. Sade should wait there, she said, for Miss Harcourt, who would take her to her tutor group. The office lady assured Aunt Gracie that it was all right to leave. Sade would be well looked after.

"Have a good day then!" Aunt Gracie squeezed Sade's hand and left.

Sade chose to stay where she was rather than cross the hallway again. No one took any notice of her as she pressed her back to the wall. In Presentation High the teachers were very strict about uniform but some of the girls here wore makeup around their eyes and most were wearing shoes quite unlike the plain black lace-ups that Aunt Gracie had bought for her on Saturday. The thick heels made them look taller. A couple of girls wore smartly shaped boots. There were a variety of anoraks and coats, many not even the navy stipulated in the school uniform list. All around her, conversations bubbled, sometimes with loud laughter. But there was too much of a clamor for Sade to understand what anyone was saying. It amazed her that the students were allowed to make so much noise. When the office lady told them to move away, the students shifted only slightly.

All weekend Sade had been wondering what it would be like to be in a high school with boys as well as girls. But the girls here seemed just as noisy and casual as the boys and it was the girls who appeared to take the most liberties with uniform.

The hubbub waned only after the screeching of a bell. Most of the students began to drift away down a corridor although a few still stayed chatting. Suddenly the deputy head's door opened and a voice boomed across the entrance hall like a cannon in rapid fire.

"What do you think that bell was for? A tongue-wagging marathon? Where are you all meant to be?"

No one looked upset. Students simply turned and began to walk away, some even grinning. The deputy head glanced over to Sade.

"What are you doing here? Why aren't you in class?" Sade stood petrified. "Oh, yes . . . you're the new girl, aren't you? Where is Miss Harcourt? She'll show you to your tutor group."

Miss Harcourt arrived carrying a large pile of books. If it had been Miss Okoya, Sade would have offered to carry them right away.

"Sorry to be late!" Miss Harcourt was out of breath. "There are always a hundred and one things to do. You'll think it's a bit of a madhouse at first! But I'm sure you'll soon get used to it. Follow me."

It was hard work keeping up with Miss Harcourt's brisk pace. Along the corridor, through a couple of large double doors and then up two flights of stairs and down another long corridor, passing classrooms on either side. Outside a closed door at the end, Miss Harcourt turned to Sade. The sound of loud chatter carried out into the corridor.

"This is your tutor group—8M. Mr. Morris is your tutor and also your English teacher. Any help you need, just ask him."

Sade kept her gaze just below Miss Harcourt's intense green eyes. Today her trouser suit was the same color as her ruby lipstick.

"Of course you can also come to me. I take a special interest in children from other countries and help some of them with their English. I'll ask one of them to show you around and help you settle in. I'm sure you'll make lots of other friends soon."

Miss Harcourt was trying to make her feel at ease, but the more she said that she was sure, the less sure Sade felt about anything. Miss Harcourt signaled her to stay outside, while she opened 8M's door.

"Can I have a quick word with Mariam, please, Mr. Morris, before I introduce your new class member?"

A girl with a navy blue headscarf, sweater and trousers came out of the room. Her face reminded Sade of the Sand-Dunes Lady who had been cradling her baby in the Immigration Office.

"This is Mariam, one of my best students. Aren't you, Mariam?"

Mariam smiled shyly as Miss Harcourt explained that she would like her to look after Sade.

"I can help her, miss." Her forehead wrinkled as she added, "No problem!" Both the girl and Miss Harcourt laughed.

"Mariam came from Somalia, less than a year ago. So, East and West Africa! I'm sure you'll become good friends."

Opening the door to the classroom, Miss Harcourt ushered them in.

"Mr. Morris, I'd like you and 8M to meet Sade Adewale —"

Sade heard no more. If she had been thrown onto a stage in front of a thousand people, she could not have felt more embarrassed.

Don't show people when you are frightened. Don't let them see it.

Mama's words came to her almost as if her mother were standing right behind her, whispering into her ear. She must look up, ahead of her, not down at the floor. Slowly she forced herself to raise her head, lifting her eyes above the line of desks, sweaters, shirts and ties. There, in among the sea of faces, waiting to catch her attention, was Kevin Graham. He was smirking.

CHAPTER 21

"WHAT KIND OF NAME IS THAT?"

SADE SLID INTO THE SEAT NEXT TO MARIAM, two rows away from Kevin. The bell screeched again but, as their first lesson was English with Mr. Morris, 8M did not have to change classrooms.

"Take out your draft books, 8M! You're going to be writing!" Mr. Morris appeared to be using a lot of energy to make his voice heard. He was a slim man with a pale narrow face and a long bony nose below metal-rimmed glasses. He crossed the room to bring Sade a blue exercise book.

"Write your name on the front. I'll speak to you later," he said with a hurried smile.

Sade was in the middle of writing her name when a head of spiky blond hair poked between her and Mariam and withdrew.

"Can't spell her own name!" Sade heard the clear whisper. "Miss said 'Sha-day' and she ain't put in no 'h'!"

"Don't need to spell in the bush!"

Sade gripped her pen as a small explosion of laughter rippled behind her.

"Donna and Marcia, stop that chattering! You're meant—

if you had listened—to be getting your books out." Mr. Morris sounded tired even though it was the first lesson of the day.

"We only wanted to know, sir, what the new girl's name means."

"Remember you told us about African customs, sir. You know, long names. How they all have different meanings and that!"

"Well, it is not the time now for continuing that discussion. Get your books out. Hurry! That goes for you too, Kevin Graham!"

Sade felt that eyes were on her, all around. The girls immediately behind her were still talking to each other under their breath. It was a relief when Mr. Morris finally began the lesson. They were to write about a place that had been very special to them when they were younger. He wanted them to use words that made other people feel they could see, hear, even smell their special place.

"Oh, that's disgusting, sir!" one of the girls behind Sade called out.

"And why is that, Marcia?" Mr. Morris' voice contained a note of irritation.

"Because my best place was at my granny's in Jamaica. It was great except for the smells, sir. My granny keeps cows and they make a terrible pong, sir!" the girl whined. The class exploded into laughter and Mr. Morris had to shout for quiet. Even Mariam smiled a little and Sade turned her head just enough to see who Marcia was. A girl with honey-brown skin, bold eyes and a pouting mouth sat directly behind Mariam. Her sleek dark hair was pulled back except for two slender plaits, knotted with purple beads, which hung from each side of her forehead.

Mr. Morris continued the lesson by reading a poem. It was about a man stopping with his little horse in the middle of a forest with snow falling, getting deeper and deeper. Snow was something Sade had only heard about and seen on television. She was surprised at the quiet picture that came into her head of the man all alone among the trees with his horse.

Afterward, Mr. Morris asked questions about some of the words the poet had used. It was the first time that Sade had heard of Robert Frost and she liked the poem. His name even seemed to fit. When it was time for them to start their own writing, Mr. Morris said that he wanted them to work in silence.

"Use your own inner eyes and ears," he reminded them.

"What about inner noses, sir?" The voice was Kevin's and was followed by sniggering around the class.

"Don't start that nonsense again, thank you, Mr. Graham. Just get on with your work!"

"Aaaah, sir! That's not fair! It's a proper question!" Kevin moaned in the same tone he used with his mother. This triggered another bout of whispering behind Sade.

"Only answers his favorites!"

"Yeah! Bet this new Africa girl will be one!"

"Marcia and Donna, if I have to speak to you once more, I shall separate you." Mr. Morris glared at them as he walked up to Sade's desk.

"Do you understand what you have to do?" he asked her. She nodded.

"Good. Miss Harcourt says your English is excellent. I look forward to seeing your work," Mr. Morris said with an encouraging smile.

If she could bury herself in writing, she could forget everything else for a while. Sade knew exactly what she wanted to write about. The forest behind Family House. Papa had once got lost in it as a boy and she and Femi were only allowed to play at the forest edges in sight of the village. Even so, it was mysterious and wonderful. How could she ever find words to describe the extraordinary shapes and colors in that tangle of branches and leaves? Or what it felt like to hide in a homemade den surrounded by a thicket of shadows? Or to glimpse slivers of sky through razor-edged palm leaves so high above you that they looked stark black? It was with wood from this forest that her own desk had been made. By special order from Papa. He had wanted her to have a memory of the forest in her bedroom in the city. Mama had crocheted her a little white mat for it. So the desk wouldn't be stained whenever she brought Sade a drink.

"Don't you like to write?" Mariam enquired softly. Sade glanced around. Everyone she could see, including Mariam, appeared to have started. The more she had thought about the forest, the less she knew where to begin. But she was saved by the bell.

"I haven't dismissed you yet," called Mr. Morris as the low hum of voices became an instant roar. Struggling to establish silence again, he announced that as so much time had been wasted, he wanted everyone to complete their description for homework.

"Did you see the way he looked at us?" Donna griped. "It's not the night for English homework anyway!"

"Yeah, it's not fair. I'm not doing it. No one's doing it. You pass that on!" Marcia ordered.

At break, Mariam showed Sade to the girls' cloakroom.

"I wait for you here," she said, pointing to the corridor. Sade pushed open the door, leaving Mariam outside.

"Oi, Marcia, look who's here!" Donna and two other girls were by the sink.

"Who?" Marcia's voice came from behind one of the toilet doors. Sade's instinct told her to leave. But Donna had already slipped between her and the cloakroom door. She had put something on her eyelashes that made her pupils into little blue pools each surrounded by a circle of black, rather sticky ferns.

"What's your name again?" she demanded cheekily. "Marcia wants to know." Sade pressed her lips together. She was aware of the other two girls closing in on her. A chain flushed and a lock was unbolted.

"Miss Harcourt says your English is excellent!" Marcia mimicked Mr. Morris. She leaned against the cloakroom door next to Donna and folded her arms. With her stacked heels she was taller than Sade.

"So you'd better tell us. What—is—your—name?" She bounced the words like she was skimming a sharp stone over water, waiting to see it hit her target. Sade felt trapped.

"Sade . . . Adewale," she said slowly, forcing herself to look at Marcia.

Don't let them see you're afraid.

"Sha-day-aday what?" Marcia drawled. "What kind of name is that then?"

"Nigerian." Sade tightened her fist on her rucksack strap.

"How come you speak English then?" Donna asked pertly. Sade knew they weren't interested. They wanted to play with her until they grew tired.

"We have lots of languages. One of them is English." She couldn't stop the edge of curtness in her voice.

"Well, just don't come and show off to us, Miss Sha-day-aday," Marcia scowled. "Didn't your mum teach you manners in Africa?"

Sade said nothing. How dare they talk about Mama!

"She sounds better when she shuts up, hey, Marcia!" snorted one of the other girls.

"You heard what I said about the English homework, right?" Marcia continued loftily. "No one does it. No one. Not unless I say so."

"Everyone listens to Marcia in 8M," Donna confided, as if now offering friendly advice. "If you don't, you'll have her to deal with. And if that's not enough for you, you'll have her brother too!" She laughed and the others joined her. "Then you can really feel sorry for yourself!"

Flicking her braids, Marcia led her troupe out of the cloakroom. As soon as they had gone, Mariam entered, her face clouded with worry. She seemed relieved to see Sade.

"They bad girls," she said nervously. "They make trouble. They don't like Africans. I don't know why."

An uneasy thought suddenly lodged itself in Sade's mind.

Why had Mariam stayed outside? Had Marcia told her to bring Sade to this particular cloakroom—so they could get her alone? Or was it just accident? She knew nothing about Mariam. But one thing was fairly sure. Mariam was frightened of Marcia. Others were probably too. There had been no student like her at Presentation High. No one with so much power. Was it really true that Marcia decided whether 8M did their homework or not? And—more to the point—was she going to let Marcia dictate to her now?

CHAPTER 22

BULLIES IN THE HEAD

A FRESHLY BAKED CHOCOLATE CAKE was waiting on the kitchen table when Sade arrived back at the Kings'. A large slice was already missing. Sade called to Femi who was huddled in front of the television next door. He didn't reply.

"Femi won't talk to me too, you know. But at least he likes my baking! I decided you both deserve a treat after your first day at school," Aunt Gracie said brightly. Sade didn't feel like talking either but it was difficult not to respond. Aunt Gracie was trying so hard to make them feel at home.

They sat together for a short while in the warm kitchen. Splashes of color in among the crockery and a tray of pink and white flowers on the windowsill defied the grayness outside.

"How was it at school?" Aunt Gracie poured orange juice for Sade and tea for herself. Ever since morning break, Sade had not been able to get Marcia's threat out of her mind. They were in different classes for math and science, but at lunchtime, Marcia and Donna had sauntered across the canteen to the table next to her and Mariam. The small group with them included Kevin. Sade had tried not to look but she felt sure the titters of laughter were about her, especially

126

when she heard snatches of Kevin's voice and something about wearing other people's clothes. Why had they taken such instant dislike to her? Mariam said they didn't like Africans. It was a puzzle. Marcia said her grandmother lived in Jamaica. Didn't she know—like the Kings did—that her own ancestors came from Africa?

Aunt Gracie's right eyebrow was raised like a question mark, waiting.

"How was it?" she repeated. "Any problems?"

"It was fine, thank you," Sade replied. She hardly tasted the soft crumbling chocolate. As soon as the lie was out of her mouth, she remembered Mama's *Tell a lie, play with fire. But don't complain of the smoke.*

She finished her cake and drink, only half listening as Aunt Gracie spoke about her first school. It had been little more than a shed, ruled over by a teacher who carried his cane everywhere. When Aunt Gracie asked if she had homework, Sade nodded. Two other teachers besides Mr. Morris had given them work.

"Why not go upstairs, mi dear, and do it before supper? No time like the present, you know!"

Sade was glad to enter the quiet of her room. For a while she sat at the desk in the growing dark with the pineapple curtains pulled back, watching the evening shadows gradually swamp over the back gardens. Some of the houses on the far side of the gardens became hidden in the dusk while glowing squares and rectangles lit up others. In a strange way the darkness reminded her of the forest she had intended writing about. The patches of light reminded her that other human beings were out there too. It was a bit like being able to glimpse the village and Family House from their hideout at the forest's edge. But there you knew the people—and who were your friends. Here you didn't know who was within those squares of lights and whether they would be friendly. What if one of them was Marcia's house? Even if you were being threatened by something terrible in the shadows out there, you wouldn't want to knock on her door!

Sade pulled the curtains across the window, turned on the lamp by her desk and removed her English book from her bag. Why was she letting Marcia frighten her so much? The girl probably tried to push her weight around with every new student, making them believe that she was in charge. Her threat was probably a big joke. Marcia and Donna would just love to watch her getting into trouble with Mr. Morris because she hadn't done her work. Well, they weren't going to catch her out.

When Aunt Gracie called Sade to the telephone just before supper, all her homework was finished. Mama Appiah was ringing to find out about their first day at school.

"It was fine, thank you." This time the words didn't seem like such a lie. It was also easier saying them into a telephone.

"Did you make any friends today?" Mama Appiah delved a little further.

"There's a girl—she's called Mariam. She sat with me." Femi had come out to the hallway to listen. Holding on to the bannisters with one hand, he swung his body in slow semi-circles.

"Ah, a Somali name!"

"Yes, my teacher said."

"Mmm. Probably a refugee too." Mama Appiah's tone was matter-of-fact but it injected a question into Sade's mind. Had something dreadful happened to Mariam and her family as well? Mama Appiah went on to enquire about Femi, but when Sade held out the receiver to him, he turned away and wandered back into the sitting room. Reminding Sade that their immigration questionnaire had still to be filled in, Mama Appiah said that she would take the children next week for a further interview with Mr. Nathan.

That night Sade dreamed she was answering the telephone in Papa's study.

The voice is Donna's. It is giggling, threatening her with Marcia and her brother. Papa grabs the receiver but the voice is no longer there.

"Bullies are cowards!" he says dismissively.

There is fierce knocking at the gate. Joseph runs to open it and Mama hurries behind him. Marcia is standing there, pointing at Sade.

"That's her!" she calls over her shoulder.

Two sharp cracks splinter the air. She hears her father's fierce cry, rising, falling.

"No! No!"

The revving of a car and skidding of tires smothers his voice.

"Mama mi?" Sade whispers.

Marcia looks loftily down at Sade crouching beside Mama.

"It was meant for you!"

Sade's eyes searched fearfully through the shadows of the bedroom while her fingers groped for the lamp switch. Even with the light on, she continued to shiver. The little white alarm clock with green numbers, which Aunt Gracie had placed on her desk, showed that it was just past three o'clock. She squeezed herself, almost pinching, rubbing her arms. What was wrong with her? Why was she letting Marcia sneak inside her head and frighten her so much? She hardly knew her and yet here was the girl already in her dreams, mixed up in her nightmare about Mama. If she could talk with Papa, she could imagine what he would say. At least what he would have said before Mama died.

We have to stand up to bullies, Sade girl! Otherwise they get inside your head. That's how they succeed in controlling us. The Bully-Boy Soldiers rule us today because most people let them. They frighten us into believing they are all-powerful. Without their brass buttons they are nothing.

Everything Papa said was true. But what happens when you stand up alone yet everyone else is too frightened? That's what she wanted to ask him. What would he say now . . . after what they did to Mama? And what if some people actually blamed Papa? They might say, Look, it was your fault. If you had kept quiet, like everyone else, your wife wouldn't have been killed. Your children wouldn't have lost their mother.

Sade's mind suddenly jumped to Uncle Tunde's face as he accused Papa.

"You call your article 'Our Children's Future.' What do you

imagine will happen now to your own, Folarin?"

Then the next moment her uncle and father were agreeing that Uncle Dele would look after the children in London. But would they have still sent them in the airplane with that awful Peacock Lady if they had known Uncle Dele had gone missing? Where on earth was he? Sade tossed and turned. Too many awful questions were scurrying into her brain. As if she had trodden on a nest of giant ants and they were crazily trying to reassemble themselves. In desperation she reached up to the shelf for the *Girls' Annual*. Pulling her quilt securely around her, she absorbed herself in the adventures of two girls lost on Dartmoor while searching for runaway ponies. The next story was about a girl sent away to boarding school when her mother becomes seriously ill. Sade kept reading until her eyes began to ache. It was after four o'clock when at last she switched off her lamplight and fell into a heavy sleep.

CHAPTER 23

"MARCIA WANTS YOU!"

WHEN MRS. KING OFFERED to accompany the children to school, Sade assured her that they would be fine on their own. Neither child spoke as they walked except when Sade said good-bye outside Greenslades' high wire fencing. Femi did not even turn around to look at her and she felt hurt. Her nightmare had made her unsure about defying Marcia. But now that she had done the homework, at least if she saw everyone else handing theirs in, she could hand hers in too. On the other hand, if all the rest of the class hadn't actually done it, she needn't admit that she had. It certainly wouldn't do to stand out as the goody-goody.

A red double-decker bus hurtled past with Avon students clustered on the platform, ready to get out at the next stop. Sade levered her scarf higher up her neck. The wind was bitingly cold. It felt as if wings with frozen feathers were being brushed against her cheeks. At the main gate she joined the stream of students tramping up the drive. Mariam had said they were allowed go to their tutor room first thing in the morning as Mr. Morris was often in early. But what if he asked her about her homework before their English lesson? She wouldn't yet know if the others had done the work or not. She slowed her pace in spite of the cold.

With her head bent down as she approached the entrance doors, Sade first saw the black tights and stacked shoes that blocked her way. Looking up, she found herself staring directly at the black sticky ferns around Donna's blue-pool eyes.

"Marcia wants you."

Before Sade could say anything, their arms were linked together and she was being marched away from the entrance toward the far end of the building.

Around the corner was a covered area under which Marcia and her gang huddled between a couple of concrete pillars. Kevin was there as well as another boy she didn't recognize and the two girls from the cloakroom. Kevin took a couple of quick puffs at a cigarette stub, then passed it on to one of the girls.

"You made us stay out in the cold! Did it on purpose, didn't you?" said Marcia. "You knew we'd be waiting for you, right?"

Sade didn't reply. She was their captive but they couldn't make her speak.

"Thought you said you'd taught her about manners, hey, Marcia?" the second boy sneered.

"Well, have you done your English then?" Marcia jutted her chin out toward Sade as Donna yanked the rucksack off her shoulder. The two boys jumped forward to help and Sade stared helplessly as they pulled at the clips. Within seconds her English book lay open in Marcia's hands. She flicked over the pages.

"Neat writing! Five pages! Ooh, won't Mr. Morris be pleased!" Marcia oozed sarcasm. The others laughed and her tone switched.

"You reckoned I wasn't serious, right? Well, let me tell you, girl, I mean what I say. When I said no one was going to do that homework without my say-so, I was talking about YOU!" With a flourish Marcia ripped out the first two pages in Sade's book. "YOU are NO ONE. Get it? No one."

Sade watched the neat lines of her handwriting crumple as Marcia squashed the pages into a tight ball. Marcia bounced it up in the air a couple of times before flinging it away carelessly onto the tarmac. Sade's eyes tingled and she fought to hold back her tears. That's what they were waiting for. Bending down she fiddled with the clips on her rucksack.

"Lost your tongue, have you? Well you better keep it lost. I haven't finished with you yet. D'you hear?"

Sade didn't reply to Marcia. All she wanted was to get away from the prying eyes and to retrieve the ball of paper being rolled across the tarmac by the wind. But if she went after it, one of Marcia's gang was sure to grab it back.

The bell saved her, drawing attention away from her and starting new chatter.

"See you around, Sha-day-aday!" Donna giggled as the group ambled off toward the front of the school. As soon as they had disappeared around the corner, Sade ran to scoop up the ball of paper. She was shaking. How could she face going into the class now? If it wasn't so cold she would have been tempted to slip out of the school gates. But she didn't fancy wandering around on the streets in this weather. Anyway, wouldn't people wonder what a child in uniform was doing not in school? Nor could she go back to the Kings' without explaining what had happened. Perhaps Aunt Gracie would want to come to the school to complain. Life with Marcia would surely become even worse if Sade got her into trouble.

Without opening the scrunched-up paper, Sade stuffed it into her bag. Reluctantly she followed in the footsteps of Marcia's gang back to the main entrance. Her shoes clattered in the silence of the empty hallway as she hurried toward the corridor and the stairs. She was late. From the top of the stairs she could see that 8M's door was shut and that she was going to have to enter the classroom in full view of everyone again.

Mr. Morris frowned but his brow seemed to relax a little when he saw who it was.

"Have you been lost?" he asked.

Sade didn't want to lie. Instead she nervously bit her lip and Mr. Morris didn't pursue his question.

"Go and sit down. You'll soon find your way around," he said tolerantly.

"Teacher's pet!" Donna whispered loudly as Sade approached her seat. Sade avoided looking directly at anyone, including Mariam.

A little later, when Mr. Morris called for the English homework to be handed in, Donna offered to collect the books.

"That's a pleasant change. Thank you, Donna!" Mr. Morris sounded pleased. Grinning, Marcia's friend strode over to the other end of the room so that their own column of desks would be the last. Sade hung down her head, waiting. She was aware of the other students taking out their books and she ignored Mariam's nudgings to do the same. She knew what was going to happen. Donna arrived and stuck out her palm in front of Sade's face. When Sade didn't respond she called out.

"Sir! The new girl hasn't done it, sir! Maybe she doesn't understand English properly, sir?"

"There's no need to shout, Donna. Just collect the rest, thank you," replied Mr. Morris. The chattering around the classroom suddenly quietened and Sade sensed that the teacher was walking over to her desk.

"I'm disappointed. I was looking forward to reading your work. What happened?" His voice was low and calm. When Papa or one of her teachers spoke to her like that, it always touched her more deeply than if they shouted.

Her tongue felt as heavy as Grandma's old-fashioned iron. Her head remained lowered.

"Well, make sure you hand it in tomorrow then. I expect everything is still rather new to you," Mr. Morris said quietly.

"You wouldn't let me get away with it, would you, sir? I'd get detention! Is it 'cause she's a girl, sir?" Sade recognized Kevin's whine.

"No, stupid!" Marcia hissed. "It's 'cause she's African. Sir wouldn't let me get away with it either!"

As Mr. Morris brought the class to quiet, Sade felt Mariam's fingers press lightly on her arm. She flinched, curling inwards. She felt as scrunched-up as her handwriting on the ball of paper that Marcia had flung so carelessly into the wind. But what could you do when you were up against people who told powerful lies?

CHAPTER 24

A DISTANT SILENCE

FOR THE REST OF THE WEEK Marcia and her gang ignored Sade completely. Whenever Marcia passed her—in the dinner queue, corridor, classroom or playground—she stared right through Sade, as if she wasn't there. After what had already happened, this disturbed Sade even more. She could feel herself becoming more timid, like a small creature whose ears and eyes were always in a state of alarm. If only she could be like the smart little rabbit in Mama Buki's stories who always managed to trick the bigger animals. Of course Mama would have advised her to ignore Marcia and her friends as much as she could, to keep out of their way.

There is no medicine to cure hatred.

But she could also imagine Papa saying *"That might be true, Mama, but sometimes even children have to stand up to bullies. If they don't, those bullies put on even bigger boots!"*

If only Papa were here with them, she could confide in him. Perhaps he would know why Marcia and her gang had taken such immediate dislike to her. She couldn't work it out. Why did they go on about Africa so much? What had Africans done to them? Or maybe they disliked her because

137

of something else altogether. Sade's anxiety about Marcia kept growing. In her nightmares, just as Papa could not stop Mama being shot, he could not prevent Marcia from entering their yard and pointing her accusing finger at Sade. But with each passing day without news of their father, Sade began to feel even more fearful whenever she thought of Papa.

One evening, Mama Appiah called to see them. The Art College still had no news of Uncle Dele but she had a suggestion. If they could give details of their home address, the International Red Cross might be able to help put them in touch with their family. Sade panicked. She had already lied about their surname and their home town! So far Mama Appiah and Mr. Nathan only knew that there had been some trouble with the government. Sade was dreading the next interview with Mr. Nathan when they had to begin filling in their Asylum Questionnaire. Until Papa was safely out of Nigeria, it would surely be dangerous if the Red Cross started asking questions. In the meantime, what could they say? It was as if she and Femi were caught inside a thicket of twine and branches with Papa somewhere outside. They dare not even shout to let him know where they were in case the noise alerted the guards who wanted to capture him. Mama Appiah must have seen the alarm in Sade's face. The children didn't have to decide right away, she said. They could think about her suggestion and tell her when she came to take them to Mr. Nathan.

On Sunday afternoon, Sade decided to ask if they could try to ring their uncle in Lagos. They were all in the sitting room with Aunt Gracie knitting, Uncle Roy reading the weekend papers and Femi as usual in front of the television.

"Your uncle? But of course, mi dear!" Aunt Gracie was in the middle of a row but put down her knitting needles.

Femi's face showed nothing but Sade felt her own cheeks burning at the lie.

"You'll need the code." Uncle Roy's grave eyes viewed Sade over the top of his paper. Sade nodded nervously. They would have to pretend with Aunt Gracie just as they had done with Mrs. Graham.

In the hallway, Aunt Gracie looked on anxiously as Sade held the receiver. Femi slunk in silently beside her. A series of clicks, followed by a long silence, was suddenly broken by the sound of distant ringing. Even Femi's eyes became alert. Sade willed someone to pick up the telephone. Surely, at least Joseph was there. As before, she planned to speak about Papa in Yoruba so Aunt Gracie would not be able to understand. The ringing continued. The more Sade held on, the farther away it seemed to be. Like a lighthouse flickering in the distance, so far away that you might even be imagining it. Femi slouched back into the sitting room. In the end, the ringing cut off itself and Sade had to replace the receiver. Aunt Gracie put a comforting arm around her.

"Never mind. We'll try later. It only means that your uncle is out."

But when they tried again that night, it was the same. A telephone ringing endlessly in an empty room. This time Uncle Roy joined them. He was such a tall man that the hallway felt crowded and Sade felt doubly nervous.

"What kind of work does your uncle do?"

"He's . . . a lawyer."

Sade saw Femi glance at her strangely. She didn't see why she should make up a lie about Uncle Tunde.

"Do you know where he works in Lagos? We might try him there, you know." Uncle Tunde had an office but Sade had no idea where it was.

"We could try the International Directory Inquiries," suggested Aunt Gracie. "If your uncle has his own office, we might find it that way. What do you think?" Her voice rose with hope.

"All right, Auntie," Sade replied, uncertainly.

"He's your daddy's brother, did you say? Shall I ask then for Mr. Adewale?"

Sade did not contradict Aunt Gracie. When Aunt Gracie asked for his first name, she replied that it was Tunde. Short for Olatunde. At least that was true.

As Sade listened to Aunt Gracie's long conversation with the operator, she felt sick. She was wasting everyone's time. Her lie was like a dirty spoon sinking into honey. When Aunt Gracie finally gave up, Sade hoped her face did not show her relief. But when Uncle Roy suggested that they pass on the information about Uncle Tunde to the International Red Cross, she was trapped all over again. Suddenly she understood Femi's blankness. It was his way of cutting himself off from all the useless thoughts and questions that cluttered her brain. Femi wasn't even trying to make sense of things. But this was too much for her to sort out alone. She had to talk with him. Make him talk to her. They were both in the same mess. Even if he had no suggestions, at least he could listen. It wasn't fair for him to blank everything out and leave her to do all the worrying.

"Good-night, mi dear. We'll think of something, don't worry!" Aunt Gracie gave Sade a small hug.

"Thank you, Auntie. Good-night." Sade tried to smile. One hand on the banisters, she leaped up two stairs at a time. Without knocking on Femi's door, she turned the handle softly and slipped in. Femi was already in bed, reading a comic. He scowled at her.

"Femi, I want to talk with you," she whispered, sitting down at the lower end of his bed. Her brother produced a loud irritated click.

"Please, Femi. You're the only one who knows the—"

Before she had even finished, she felt a kick under the quilt.

"Shut up! I don't want to hear!"

"But . . ." Sade stopped. There was no point going on. Femi's eyes glinted angrily. He detested her along with everything else. Her lips quivering, Sade fled to her room.

CHAPTER 25

STRANGLEHOLD

ON MONDAY MORNING, Sade intended to walk ahead of Femi as they set off for school. The Yellow Jacket Lady would see him across the main road outside his school. Femi had said nothing to her at breakfast, avoiding even looking at her. But a quick glimpse into his eyes, as he opened the wooden gate on to the pavement, revealed such deep wells of misery that she immediately felt sorry for him. It was pointless asking what was wrong. She slowed her pace to his.

They were approaching Femi's school when Sade thought she heard "Sha-day-aday!" shouted above the rumble of traffic. Femi must have heard something too because he swung around swiftly toward the road. Sade kept her head down against the wind. She made a point of not looking up into the throng of Avon students on the platform of the passing bus.

"Are they your friends?" Femi broke his silence as the bus disappeared around a bend. Sade pulled a face. He looked as if he might ask her something else but then the barriers slid down as abruptly as they had lifted.

Sade stood for a minute watching Femi tag behind a flock of children entering the playground. Inside, children stood chattering while others scurried around yelling and chasing. Some boys and a girl were kicking a football. They dashed across the middle of the tarmac, occasionally hurtling between the others. Femi appeared to take no notice as, with his rucksack humped tortoiselike on his back, he paced slowly around the edge. The other children could have been trees or outcrops of rock from the way he skirted around them without even a glance. None of them seemed to notice him either. Was this really her football-crazy brother who had so often boasted to his friend Kole that one day he would play for Nigeria in the World Cup? The same little boy who pleaded with Papa to put a more powerful light in the backyard so that he could practice after dusk?

Sade was still on the opposite side of the road from Avon High when Marcia and Donna stepped out from behind her.

"There's something we want to show you," declared Donna, once again linking her arm into Sade's.

"Yeah, it's important!" Marcia sidled up on her other side.

"I don't want to see anything. Excuse me," Sade said tensely, making her limbs rigid as she felt herself being turned around. An elderly man hobbled past and a group of older Avon students were approaching them. Surely these two girls couldn't force her to go with them in full view of everyone?

"Excuse me!" Donna's voice tinkled with laughter as if Sade had just told a great joke.

"Look here, we were only going to do you a favor. Show you something. Help you pass the test." Marcia was matter-of-fact as she twirled one of her slim braids between her fingers.

"I told you she wouldn't know about the test!" Donna bantered. "Even if you don't come with us, you'll still have to do it, you know!"

The Avon students had passed by them, absorbed in conversation, taking no notice of Marcia, Donna, and Sade.

"Test?" Sade mumbled. "What test?"

"Right, Marcie! Let's show her. Top speed. We don't want to be late for Morrissy, do we Sha-day-aday?" Donna giggled. Sade was propelled around and found herself being marched so rapidly that they were practically jogging down the road. She was being towed between the two girls, almost like a rag doll. They stopped at the first junction.

"See down there," said Marcia, pointing with her chin. She was about half a head taller than Sade so that her chin was in line with Sade's eyes. "See that corner shop?"

Marcia indicated a small shop with a blue sign over the door at the far end of the block.

"That belongs to your friend's uncle."

"You know, your friend from Africa—what's her name?— the one you go round with." Marcia put a hand on her hip, as if explaining anything to Sade was a chore. "You tell her, Donna, what's she's got to do."

"Well, there's a really nice turquoise lighter in there." Donna lowered her voice. "Marcia fancies it. You know what a lighter is, don't you? For ciggies, right?"

Sade stared at a crushed plastic bottle lying in a little stream of dirty gutter water. She remained silent.

"Yeah, I want the turquoise one. You can get it for me."

"I don't have money to buy it." Sade said bluntly. The

force in her voice surprised her.

"That's your problem, not mine," Marcia tapped her foot impatiently. "If you don't get it for me, there'll be trouble—and not just for you, you know!"

"Excuse me?" Sade confronted Marcia's gaze. For a fleeting second Marcia's eyes wavered before resettling on her prey.

"That was your brother, right? Outside the kiddies' school, yeah?"

A spasm shot through Sade's stomach.

"We shouted to you from the bus, but you ignored us! You shouldn't have done that." Donna poked her face in front of Sade and fluttered her long black eyelashes. "Marcia's cousin goes to that school, right, Marcie?"

"Yeah. He's taller than me—and he does anything I say. I bet your kid brother needs looking after too. Know what I mean?"

Sade knew what she meant. Her eyes returned to the broken plastic bottle and a bent straw bobbing beside it in the gutter. The wind was making the water shiver slightly. She listened as Donna explained how they would be waiting at this same corner at exactly four o'clock for Sade to bring Marcia the little turquoise lighter.

"In case you think of trying something funny, just remember your little brother, right?" Sade squirmed as Donna put her arm over her shoulder, bringing her face close up to Sade's.

"Marcie's my best friend, but even I wouldn't like to cross her." It was her confidential tone.

"Oh come on, Donna," moaned Marcia. "Stop wasting time! You'll get us detention from Morrissy."

They let go of Sade's arms and set off ahead of her.

Sade was only vaguely aware of a car hooting at her as she crossed the entrance to a petrol station. What struck her more was how Marcia and Donna both turned around, startled. But then they burst out laughing. They came and placed themselves, one on each side of her.

"You've got to watch out for yourself, you know!" Donna cooed. "You better let Marcie and me look after you!"

Mariam must have seen Sade being escorted across the main road. She approached Sade as they were trooping up the stairs.

"What do they want?" she whispered.

"It's nothing," Sade shrugged.

Mariam didn't press further.

All morning, Sade's mind throbbed with questions. Mr. Morris asked her if she wasn't feeling very well and Sade had to say that she was fine. The math teacher gave a short lecture about daydreamers when she caught Sade staring out of the window. Sade tried to concentrate on solving the algebra problem on the board, but her mind soon wandered again. It was all very well Papa saying, *"We have to stand up to bullies! Expose them for what they are"* and *"If you allow bullies a stranglehold, they'll have you by the throat!"*

But what could you do when they already had you by the throat? Shout for help from the teachers? But would they believe her? Why had no one else told on Marcia? If she reported Marcia's threat to Mr. Morris, wasn't it even more likely that Femi would get hurt? Marcia could use her cousin to get revenge. They might even do something out of school. It wouldn't be hard for Marcia to find out where they lived.

At lunchtime Sade went with Mariam to the library. It was warm inside and the librarian was friendly. Marcia and her gang were unlikely to come because the students were not allowed to make a lot of noise there. Sade followed Mariam to a table tucked between some shelves, each taking a book from a wire stand. Sade chose one with a cover that had a face looking into a cracked mirror in which there was a cracked face. Girl or boy? She wasn't sure, but terror was written all over that face. Mariam's book showed a dark-haired girl in a headscarf looking toward distant mountains. Last week, Sade had seen Mariam spend most of her time in the library studying the cover of the same book. Perhaps the picture allowed her to dream. Today Sade took the chance to ask Mariam about her family. She knew she was asking for the wrong reasons, but the minutes were ticking by toward four o'clock and she needed to find out about Mariam's uncle and his shop. What Mariam told her left her feeling quite numb.

CHAPTER 26

NO ESCAPE

WHEN MRS. HOWE, the librarian, asked if either of them could help her sort some books for a short while after school, Mariam offered to stay for half an hour. She only lived around the corner. Anything later and her mother and uncle would become worried. Sade fumbled over her excuse. Her brother would be waiting for her outside his school. It wasn't true, but Mrs. Howe said she quite understood.

A lie has seven winding paths, the truth one straight road.

Sade quashed Mama's voice in her head by calculating the time it would take Mariam to get from school to her uncle's shop. If Mariam saw her with Marcia's gang after school, she would surely suspect something. But if Mariam stayed in the library until four, she might just miss bumping into them.

Had Sade been asked that afternoon why she was going to give in to Marcia's threats, especially after what Mariam told her about her family, she would surely have broken down. If Papa had only been there, she would have gone to him. However much she would have cried and sobbed about Marcia this and Marcia that, they would have made a plan.

She could even imagine Papa going to talk to Marcia's parents, to the cousin and of course to Marcia herself. Papa would have made Marcia see reason.

Where the water rules, the land submits.

But she was on her own. Just like the child on the book cover, looking into the mirror and a face cracked into a thousand pieces. That lonely terror was hers too. There was only one thing to do. However hurt she was by Femi shouting at her, shutting her out, he was still her little brother. Hadn't Mama and Papa always expected more of her because she was older? If she didn't do what Marcia wanted and Marcia's cousin beat Femi up, she would be to blame. She had to steal the turquoise lighter so Femi would not be harmed. Perhaps then they would leave her alone. Once she had proved herself, what more could they want?

After the final bell, Mariam seemed anxious to say something to Sade before going up to the library.

"I don't tell about my—my family to everyone. But you are my friend, OK?"

Mariam's eyes searched Sade's face for a response. They were timid yet strangely brave. At any other time, Sade would have felt good that Mariam had trusted her. This afternoon it made her feel worse.

"It's OK," she said, almost curtly. "I have to go. See you tomorrow." She tried to smile but was actually pressing her lips together to cover her agitation.

Marcia and Donna had indicated that Sade was to go into the shop by herself. Now all she wanted was to get the thing over and done with. She squeezed through the crowd of students at the bus stop and hurried down the main road. This time she took in the petrol station and the row of shops on her left. Through the windows she could see how small they were inside. No hiding places where you wouldn't be seen by the shopkeeper. She had no idea where she would find the cigarette lighters in the corner shop. They might even be in a locked cabinet. What if Marcia knew that all along and she was being set up, once again, for a trick? Perhaps she wasn't meant to succeed and Marcia was just out to grind her underfoot. Sade's heart was now juddering so fiercely, she was sure that anyone behind the counter—Mariam's uncle or her mother?—would be suspicious.

The full seriousness of what she was about to do suddenly hit her. What if she was caught stealing? The police would be called. Of course, that's what Marcia wanted! And then how would she and Femi ever get permission to stay here in England? All that asylum business with Mr. Nathan would be for nothing. The Immigration people would say she was a thief. And when Papa came, they would say they didn't want someone whose daughter was a thief! How stupid she was, falling right into Marcia's trap.

Sade stood at the junction with the corner shop just down the road. No, she was not going in there. She turned swiftly back along the main road. But before she could go anywhere, she found herself being rapidly swung around. Once again, Marcia and Donna grabbed her by the arms and within seconds were jogging her down the side road. The only other people walking in the dismal street were over in the next block, too far away to see. Even if they had been near by, they would probably have thought it was all a game.

"Thought you'd change your mind, did you? Chicken?" Marcia panted.

"Marcie and me have come to give you a hand. Thought you might be a bit nervous as it's your first time," Donna quipped.

They stopped a short way from the corner shop. Briefly Marcia explained, in a subdued voice, that she would distract the shopkeeper by buying something while Sade took the lighter from a shelf on the right-hand side. Sade would have to be quick. If there was a second person behind the counter, Donna would keep her busy.

"Nicking is easy," giggled Donna. "Anyone can do it."

Passing underneath the blue sign with the words DAUD'S STORE in neat black letters, the pounding in Sade's heart froze. A tall, gaunt woman wearing a headscarf surveyed the three of them from a door leading to the back of the shop. She had high cheekbones and Mariam's eyes. She stood with a quiet dignity. A man in a white cap and tunic was stacking papers in front of the counter. Marcia asked loudly if he could show her what kind of posh chocolates he sold because it was her mum's birthday. Donna made her way to the counter and began running her fingers along the rows of sweets. Sade saw the lady's eyes follow suit. Sade turned away, forcing herself to scan the rows of shelves to her right. Notepads, pens, scissors, sticking tape, all sorts of little gadgets and, closest to the counter, a small tray of cigarette lighters. Blue, red, silver, green, but no turquoise. She heard Marcia asking Mariam's uncle to bring down a large box of chocolates from the top shelf and Mariam's mother helped with a stool to reach up for it. Sade slipped her right hand into the tray and quickly lifted up the lighters. A turquoise one lay beneath. She clutched it silently, removed her hand and slid it into her anorak pocket on the side away from the counter. Stiffly she turned to the others.

"Nah! Not big enough!" Marcia was shaking her head. "Don't think my mum actually wants chocolates, anyway. She's on a diet, see. Maybe I'll get her some next year! Come on, Donna, let's go!"

Sade saw the look of momentary surprise in both adults' eyes. They exchanged a glance of being caught off guard, then both shifted their gaze to her. Without saying anything, Sade turned to the door. Had they seen the guilt written all over her face?

As soon as they passed beyond the window of Daud's Store, Sade thrust the lighter into Marcia's hand and ran.

"Ooh, temper!" she heard Donna remark. Sade kept running, gripping her rucksack to control its bouncing. She desperately hoped Mariam would still be in the library and wouldn't see her. But Mariam's mother and uncle would be bound to describe the three girls in Avon uniform who had come into the shop. They had probably checked to see if anything was missing near where she had been standing. Did they know exactly how many lighters should be in the tray? She began puffing for breath. That final look in the faces of Mariam's mother and uncle and their grave silence cut her to the bone.

• • •

That evening, when Sade said she had a headache and wasn't hungry, Aunt Gracie was concerned. If Sade felt the same in the morning, she might need to see the doctor. Sade went to bed early and Aunt Gracie came up to check on her. Femi also slipped in to give her one of his comics. He didn't talk much, but it was his way of saying sorry. How could she tell him that she had done something a hundred times worse to people who were refugees just like them? There was no escape from the disgust she felt at herself. She had only asked Mariam about her family to find out about her uncle and his shop so that she could steal from him. And after Mariam had told her story so simply in halting English, but in words that painted such terrible pictures, Sade had shut down her mind. But now the shutter had lifted and Mariam's words and pictures were burningly clear.

CHAPTER 27

MARIAM'S STORY

FOUR SOLDIERS CAME to Mariam's house on her birthday. She was just five. Her mama had made her a cake and she was very happy, playing outside with her friends. One soldier asked, "Is Father in?" She was frightened and wanted to scream, but her voice was dead. Then her mama came to the door and cried, "What do you want?" But they pushed her away. There was no time for her father to hide. The soldiers pulled him from the house. All the children were crying. Her father was calling, "No, no. Let me walk. I will come with you. I don't want my children to see any fighting." The soldiers shouted, "You are a dog, not a man. You have been helping the rebels. We know you give them milk from your sheep." Her mother was crying. "No, no. Where are you taking him?" They said, "You will see later." That was the last time Mariam saw her father.

It was President Barre who sent the soldiers. Then the president sent his airplanes. They dropped bombs all over Hargeisa, the town where Mariam lived. A bomb fell on their house and the roof and one wall broke down. Mariam's neighbor took them in. They went to sleep on the floor underneath the beds. They kept their clothes on so they could run if they had to. Later the soldiers came back. This time they were setting fire to houses and shooting. Bullets were flying around like bees. The soldiers were killing men and boys right in front of their families. They said they were looking for rebels. The bodies were left in the street because people were too frightened to bury them. The soldiers said ten-year-old boys were helping the rebels. Mariam's mama said they must leave immediately because if the soldiers found Hassan, he would be killed. Hassan was Mariam's brother and he was ten.

Most of the men and older boys who were still alive ran away to fight. Her mama said they should go to Kenya. She told Mariam and Hassan, "It is far but we shall be safe there." People were leaving the town like water from a tap that cannot be turned off. They were mostly old people, women and children. They had to walk. Soon their legs were swollen and they were burning from the sun. After two days they started walking at night because the soldiers made roadblocks in the day. At night they heard lions roaring, but they were more frightened of the soldiers. Sometimes they passed bodies piled up at the side of the road. The smell was horrible and their mother told them, "Don't look!" But Mariam peeped through her fingers. She wished she had listened to her mama.

It seemed as if there was no end to their journey. Mariam thought her legs would drop off. Then her brother Hassan managed to buy a donkey in a village and the younger children took turns in riding it. Mariam's mama said that Hassan was now the man of the family. After some more days and nights, Mariam's mama became very ill. The pain was so bad they had to stop. Her dress was covered in blood around her legs. Some women came to help her and Mariam became scared that her mama was going to die. Later a woman told Mariam, "Your mother will be all right, but the baby is dead." She did not even know that her mother was going to have a baby. Hassan made a small hole in the dry ground. He tried to dig it deep so the animals could not get to it but the earth was hard and dry. Mariam did not know if the dead baby was a little sister or brother. She only saw a tiny bundle of cloth that was placed in the hole. Hassan covered it with dry sand.

After many days they reached Mogadishu. It was a very big place, the capital of their country. But they did not know anyone there. Mogadishu people were amazed how far they had walked. All the way across Somalia! Some Mogadishu people gave them food and told them how to find the harbor and the boats that would take them to Kenya. The boat was really frightening. Hundreds of people were packed into one small boat as if they were fish in a net. When their drinking water was finished, they almost died. One night there was a storm and the waves crashed over them. People were crying and praying because they believed they were going to drown. They were trapped in the boat for fifteen days.

The sun was rising when their boat sailed into Mombasa. They had come all the way safely to Kenya. Now people were crying and praying thanks to Allah. But when they saw soldiers by the harbor, they became quiet again. They were frightened because they had run away from soldiers. But these soldiers helped them onto trucks. They did not have to walk anymore. Their bones were aching as the trucks bumped over the roads, but they were happy to be back on land.

They reached the refugee camp at sunset. They had never seen anything like it. There were homes made out of tents and plastic sheets as far as their eyes could see. Smoke was rising everywhere from little fires. People were cooking food for the night. It looked such a strange place. Mariam cried because it was so different from their home in Hargeisa, but her mama said they were lucky to be there alive.

Mariam and her family stayed in the refugee camp for nearly six years. It was very hard, but the most terrible thing was not knowing what had happened to her father. They heard that President Barre had fled from their country but the fighting was still going on. When Mariam was eleven years old, the news began to get a little better. Her mama began to make plans to go home. Then a letter arrived that changed their lives again. It was from her father's brother in London. Charity workers had helped him find them. But he had very bad news for them. Their father had died in prison. So her uncle wanted them to come and live with him in London. He owned a small shop and he was going to look after them. He was going to work hard to get the right papers for them and then he was going to come for them. Mariam's mama agreed to his plan. She said it would give her children a chance. But when her uncle arrived, Mariam's brother Hassan refused to come to London. He said he was going back to their home in Hargeisa. He wanted to live in Somalia and he wanted to find out for himself what had happened to their father. Her mama had begged him not to go. It was still not safe. Their home had been bombed. Nothing would be left of it now. He was only sixteen. They had not heard from him since that day.

CHAPTER 28

A GUARDIAN ANGEL

SADE'S SLEEP WAS TROUBLED and her nightmare about Mama was even more distorted. Not only was Marcia there pointing at her as she crouched beside Mama's body, but this time Marcia accused her.

"It's your fault, little liar!"

But when the embroidered bedspread with its crimson stain was pulled back, Mama wasn't there. Instead a baby girl with Mariam's eyes stared lifelessly up at her.

In the morning Aunt Gracie took Sade's temperature. It was above normal and Aunt Gracie declared that she should stay in the house.

"It may just be a touch of flu, you know, but you don't look right to me, mi dear."

But when Femi complained he also wasn't feeling well, Aunt Gracie said that she was sure he would be all right once he got to school. Just as Femi seemed ready to dig his heels in, the telephone rang. It was Mama Appiah wanting to talk to them about something important. On hearing that Sade would be at home, Mama Appiah said she would call in during the morning. Femi arched his eyebrows like two bows drawn and ready to fire. But Aunt Gracie disarmed him first.

"Well, Femi, it looks like you should stay! Mrs. Appiah wants to see you both," she said.

Although her brother didn't exactly smile, Sade recognized his little look of victory.

Questions raced through Sade's head as she pulled on her tracksuit. Had the Immigration people found something wrong? Or was there news of Uncle Dele? It must be something urgent or Mama Appiah would have waited until her visit at the end of the week. But just as she was coming down the stairs, her stomach suddenly seemed to lurch beneath her. Mama Appiah had heard about her stealing the lighter! Mariam's uncle must have realized what was missing and they had worked out it was her. Mariam must have seen her after all! Then her uncle must have gone to the police, who contacted the social workers. Iyawo-Jenny had told Mama Appiah. All these people knew she was a thief! Halfway down the stairs, Sade wheeled around and scuttled back up toward her bedroom. She pushed past Femi on the landing. She slammed her door behind her. Fully clothed, she dived back into bed, burying herself deep under the quilt.

A couple of hours later, Sade sat with arms tightly folded next to Mama Appiah. Femi sat on a separate little stool. From fingertips to toes, Sade tingled with cold. The orange-blue tongues that flickered up from the gas fire that looked like coals made no difference at all. She listened to Mama Appiah agree with Aunt Gracie that "Sade doesn't seem right" and stared dully at the dancing patterns of light as Mama Appiah asked Uncle Roy and Aunt Gracie to stay in the sitting room. They too had to know that she was a thief.

"Tell me," Mama Appiah began. Sade's head curled inward, like a snail that has lost its shell. Mama Appiah and the Kings had no need to prod her. Her guilt was plain to see.

"Tell me," Mama Appiah repeated, "Sade and Femi, do you know Mr. Folarin Solaja?"

Sade's head shot up and Femi's eyes widened.

"Papa!" he cried.

Mama Appiah's eyes traveled gravely from Femi to Sade. The little bird-tails at the end of her kingfisher-blue *gele* shimmered, waiting. Sade's hand covered her mouth.

"He . . . he is our father!" The words squeezed through Sade's fingers.

"Well, truly there must be a guardian angel looking after you!" The bird-tails bobbed. "With your names Sade and Femi Adewale, your father might never have found you!"

It seemed unbelievable. Papa was already here in England! Mama Appiah had actually met him! He had told her his story. Their story. How his wife had been shot at their home in Lagos and he had sent his two children immediately to London. His younger brother was meant to take care of them. But by the time he had realized that his brother Dele was missing, the children had already been sent. He was frantically worried. He had no idea where his children were, who they were with and whether they were safe. Their names were Sade and Femi.

Sade bit her thumb so hard, it pained. But where was Papa? Why hadn't Mama Appiah brought him with her? Then the full story hit her. Yes, Papa was here, in England, but he was in detention. In prison! Femi's eyes, which had momentarily lit up, were now awash with tears. Papa had attempted to come into the country with the false passport he had to use to escape! He had been so worried about his children that all he wanted to do was to find them before asking the government for political asylum.

"I'm afraid your daddy didn't know the rules," Mama Appiah explained. "You have to tell your story—ask for asylum—the moment you arrive. If someone uses a false passport first and the immigration officers then find them out, it's too late. They won't believe their real story."

Sade was stunned. The immigration officers thought Papa was a liar!

The truth is the truth. How can I write what's untrue?

Papa, who always believed in telling the truth, had kept quiet. Until it was too late. Because he had been frantic to find his children.

Aunt Gracie slipped quietly on to the settee. She wrapped her arm around Sade, who was trembling. Femi hunched himself into a taut little figure on his stool. He had been fiercely trying to wipe his tears away.

"Tell us, Mrs. Appiah, how did you find the children's father?" Uncle Roy's bass voice steadied Sade enough to listen to the rest of Mama Appiah's story.

"A miracle! An absolute miracle, Mr. King! I had to visit a boy who has been detained by Immigration. They say he's eighteen so they locked him up. But we think he's younger."

Femi straightened up a little at the mention of the boy.

"So I went to Heathlands Detention Center where they keep detainees. Your daddy heard that someone from the Refugee Council was visiting this boy and he requested to see me. He asked if I knew two children with the surname Solaja. I said no." Mama Appiah turned to Sade. "But when he said the names Sade and Femi—and the dates fitted—I was ninety-nine percent sure it was you two."

Sade hung her head even though it was pointless trying to hide her tears. Papa was here, in England, behind bars.

"Don't blame yourself," said Mama Appiah quietly. "Sometimes people don't tell the truth because they are so desperate. I am sure that's what happened with you two and, I am very sure, with your father."

Sade's sniffs seemed much louder in her own head than Mama Appiah's voice and she strained to hear every word.

"From what he told me, I think he must be a very brave man. You must be very proud of him."

Sade detected Femi sitting up a little straighter as Mama Appiah spoke about Papa. Her mind was bobbing like a cork trapped below a waterfall.

"Do you know, Mr. and Mrs. King," Mama Appiah continued, "that these children's father is a writer? He showed me two articles. What strong words! He had to smuggle them out."

"Well, well—and these two never said a word!" Uncle Roy's voice rumbled into a deep spray of laughter.

Sade couldn't help smiling as she blinked back her tears.

● ● ●

Before leaving, Mama Appiah asked if she could ring Heathlands Detention Center to arrange a visit for the children. Sade and Femi clung nervously close as they listened to her spelling out their first names and then S-O-L-A-J-A. There was, however, yet one more surprise.

"I'd like to speak to Mr. Solaja, please," Mama Appiah asked, then held out the receiver to the children. They stared at each other in disbelief. Was it really possible that they could speak to Papa right away? While he was in prison? Sade lifted the receiver uncertainly to her ear. Tinny music was squeaking out. Then suddenly it was switched off, followed by a couple of clicks. A voice—Papa's voice—was saying "Hello."

CHAPTER 29

TERRITORY OF THE EYES

FOR THE FIRST TIME since arriving in England, Femi invited Sade to play Ayo with him. The smooth blue-brown pebbles trickled through their fingers, swooping in and out of the rows of cups carved into the wooden board. Each tried to hide their excitement and neither spoke of Papa. From Ayo they shifted to cards. Rummy and Patience.

But alone in the shadows of the night, Sade found herself adrift once again. She tossed in her bed thinking about Papa, trying to shut out memories from their last terrible day at home. Yet as soon as she blanked those out, other awful pictures slunk in. Papa lying on a narrow metal bed in a cold dark cell with only a tiny barred window for light. Someone in a white coat like Hawk Man grasping Papa's hand, forcing his fingers on to an inkpad. Handcuffs snapped onto Papa's wrists. Sade tried to chase these pictures away by recalling Papa's voice on the telephone.

Thank God you are both safe.

She had been too numb to capture the rest. Everything was jumbled in her brain. Papa speaking from inside a prison yet his words escaping like a genie from a bottle.

● ● ●

In the morning, Sade willed the hands on the clock to hurry as they waited for Mama Appiah. Femi tried to cover up his nervousness, but Sade could tell he was wound up like a spring. When at last they were seated in Mama Appiah's old beige Ford, with Femi in front and Sade behind, the car seemed painfully slow. It nudged its way through mile upon mile of crowded London streets. Even when they reached the highway, that too was choked with traffic. It was only after passing a large green sign with a white arrow pointing to Oxford that Sade felt they were finally taking off. She tapped Femi's shoulder.

"Do you remember Tortoise when he flew to the feast in the sky?"

Mama Appiah chuckled. "I know that story too! I couldn't make this old car fly even if I wanted to!"

Sade edged back into her seat as the car rattled and shook along a road that snaked between fields of brown earth and gray-green hills. The scenery outside was like a film. Or a fairy story. Nothing would be real until they saw Papa. But how strange that his prison was near Oxford!

Two enormous books stand on Papa's desk like fat generals in royal blue uniform, each with a red and green stripe on his cap. They are wedged upright between a pair of gleaming ebony Oko and Iyawo heads that are twice as large and stout as the couple on Sade's own desk. The two volumes of The Shorter Oxford English Dictionary *hold place of honor in Papa's study. Mama says that each is almost as heavy as a new-*

born baby. Treat them with care. Open them only on the table itself so their spines do not break. Sade loves the row of little fingernail half-moons slanting down along the right-hand side, each with its own gold letter of the alphabet. Papa tries to leave a small space clear of papers so the dictionary can be consulted without him being troubled. But sometimes, if he is working at his desk, he stops to ask what word she is seeking. Sade much prefers to consult "the Oxford," as they call it, rather than her school dictionary.

The name Heathlands did not sound like a prison. But when Sade and Femi clambered out into the country lane where Mama Appiah parked, they stared up at a six-meter-high wire fence topped with great loops of barbed wire. Behind the thick poles and the wire, a cluster of large brown brick buildings loomed above a tarmac yard. Every window was barred. Was Papa behind one of them? Waiting, watching. Impatiently they both searched the rows of windows, but the bars were too dense and the glass too dark to see anyone or anything.

As they approached a metal gate in the fence, there was a curious buzzing. Slowly the gate swung open as if pulled by some invisible force. A small square office overlooked the gate and, through the large plate-glass window, Sade glimpsed three figures in black and white uniforms. Once again they were entering the territory of the Eyes.

Inside, at the desk ahead of them, a visitor was arguing.

"It's only fruit for my friend! You can check it!"

"We're sorry, sir, but it's not allowed. Your friend gets fruit at mealtimes."

"Not like this! I bought pineapple and mangoes especially! Check them!"

The Eyes continued to refuse. They were polite but the answer remained no. Finally, when the man agreed to leave behind his bag of fruit, it was their turn at the desk. The Eyes and The Fingers inspected the contents of Mama Appiah's bag. Stepping through the metal-detector door frame, Sade surveyed the stretch of open tarmac leading to the next high wire barrier. Looking upward, she spotted the cameras.

They followed a guard through two further gates before entering a building with a heavily locked door. Mama Appiah shepherded the children into a large room lined with red chairs. People sat talking quietly in small groups and pairs. Anxiously Sade and Femi scanned them. Papa wasn't there.

"They'll send for your daddy now," Mama Appiah reassured. "He'll be here very soon."

It could have been a waiting room anywhere, with a machine for canned drinks in one corner. Mama Appiah had explained that Heathlands was a prison for people who wanted to live in England but who came without permission.

"It doesn't look like prison," Femi muttered to Sade.

"See there, in the corner," she whispered. There were cameras by the ceiling. The Eyes were everywhere.

They hovered close to the glass door. Through it they could watch the entrance desk where two officers sat chatting. The lady officer had smiled at the children when they entered, but neither Sade nor Femi had responded. How could they smile at Papa's jailers? Papa was locked up behind all the wire and bars just like he was a criminal. Sade kept her eyes trained on the corridor beyond the desk. Every time a figure appeared in its distant shadows, her fingernails dug deeper into her palms. Mama Appiah suggested that the children sit down, but both shook their heads, choosing to stay rooted near the door.

At last a familiar figure, but looking strangely different, came striding past the desk without even glancing at it. Toward the glass door, toward them. Papa! It was Papa, wasn't it? Behind a short beard and mustache, the face broke into a well-known smile. He pushed the glass aside and, in a great arc, his arms swept up the children. Sade felt all stiffness give way as Papa pressed them to his chest. With Papa's breath in her hair, the tears spurted hotly down her cheeks. They soaked into her father's shirt as she heard his choking voice repeat their names.

A little later, they sat on the red visitor chairs, the children on each side of Papa. There was a brief awkward silence as they struggled to find the words to begin.

"Papa, why did you grow a beard? And a mustache?" Femi wrinkled his nose. Sade wondered how her brother had managed to remain dry-eyed.

"It makes you different, Papa! I almost thought it wasn't you!" said Sade.

"You look like Uncle Tunde! It's—" Femi broke off.

"You've noticed my new gray hairs, have you?" Papa smiled. "Well, it was your uncle's idea! To change my looks as much as possible."

Their father looked thinner, especially in this narrow white shirt with buttons and not one of his usual free-flowing *agbadas*, but Sade didn't want to say it.

Papa wanted them to tell him everything. When he and Uncle Tunde had found they could not contact Uncle Dele, they had become very worried. The agent assured them that Mrs. Bankole would be taking good care of the children but said he had no way of contacting her. They suspected that he wasn't telling the truth yet there was nothing they could do except wait for the passport to be arranged.

"We tried to ring you, Papa," Sade said. "But the line was dead!"

"The police were looking for me. They cut off the phone. But now I want to hear all about you two. Until I met this good lady"—Papa's low voice almost sang the words "good lady" as he smiled at Mama Appiah—"I was almost losing my mind."

There was so much to tell Papa. Too much. Desertion at Victoria Station. The shock of Uncle Dele missing. Darth Vader of the alley grabbing their bag. Video Man accusing them and calling the police. Mrs. Graham taking them in, Kevin complaining. The awful Asylum Screening Unit . . . But also Iyawo-Jenny, Mama Appiah, Mr. Nathan . . . and of course Aunt Gracie and Uncle Roy, who were trying so hard to make them feel at home. Papa nodded with satisfaction when he heard that they were both in school. However, Sade mentioned nothing about Marcia nor about Mariam. After the earlier hugging and excitement, Femi was quieter. He said little about Greenslades Primary. Even when he was looking up at Papa, Sade thought her brother's eyes seemed lost inside him.

In the end the conversation returned to how lucky they were to have found each other again. Sade began to explain to

Papa why she had given a false surname and suddenly, without warning, she was crying again. Both Papa and Mama Appiah comforted her. All was not yet lost, they said. Mr. Nathan would take on Papa's case. He would explain to the Immigration people that Sade and Femi were actually Papa's children. He would ask them to release Papa to be with them, at least while they considered his case.

The afternoon slipped away. It came as a shock when the guard announced that all visitors had to leave. Sade hadn't yet asked anything about Mama. She hadn't yet found the words to ask where and how Mama had been buried. Nor had she brought herself to ask about Grandma. She wanted to know. Needed to know. But they were being told to go away! Femi stalked across to the door. He looked so small, tight and lonely, as if shutting himself in once again. Sade clung to Papa. Could they not stay here with him?

"I'm afraid they won't allow it."

She glimpsed a slight quivering around his mouth before the muscles tightened. Fiercely she wound her arms around him.

"Don't worry, children. This won't be for long. We shall talk on the phone. We shall be together very, very soon. We must be patient." Papa softly repeated his reassurances. But the more she heard, the tighter she held on. Papa talking about being patient didn't sound like him at all. Mama Appiah's hand lightly touched her shoulder.

"All visitors must leave right away." The guard held open the glass door. Sade wanted to shout: *"We're not visitors. This is our father."*

She shut her mind to all the words around her until gradually she felt Papa's strong fingers very gently prizing her away. The same fingers that a little while ago had been pressing her close. It was too much to bear. She let go and ran headlong toward the glass door, her sight blurred with tears, her head throbbing.

"*O dabo, Sade! O dabo, Femi!* Good-bye, Mrs. Appiah! Thank you." Papa's stifled voice followed as if from a great distance.

Unable to bear seeing Papa left by himself, Sade did not turn around.

CHAPTER 30

WANTED

6 December 1995

My dear children,

I feel very bad about the way we said good-bye. The others have gone in for the evening meal but I came back to my room to write. Of course I have no big desk here like at home. But as I sit on my bed, with the pad resting against my knees, I can see you both so clearly. Sade, I can feel your strong grip. I am reminded of Rabbit holding on to Buffalo's back for dear life so she would not drown as they crossed the river. I hated having to force your fingers to make you let go. More than anything, I want you both near me.

Femi, do you remember how you used to glare at me when you wanted us to play football but I had not finished my work? Mama would tell you to wait and I used to joke about you giving me "Bad Eye." I wish we could have played together more. But be sure, we shall play again.

I want you to know that I shall do everything possible to be free before too long. Tomorrow Mrs. Appiah will speak to Mr. Nathan and I hope he will come to see me soon. Then he can explain the truth about us to the authorities. I think they will understand why you used a different name—and why I tried to get through with the false passport. I hope they will then let me out so we can be together while they examine our request to stay here until it is safe for us to return home.

Your loving Papa

Wednesday 6 December, 11:30 p.m.

Dear Papa,

When you see the time above, you will say "Why is she not in bed sleeping?" I did try, but I just lay awake. We only got back here at nine o'clock. Auntie and Uncle were worried that we were late. But Mama Appiah said we should eat something before our journey back to London. She said hunger is a bad companion and she took us into Oxford to get fish and chips. She is very like Mama Buki. The fish and chips were good. I wish we could have shared them with you. Femi didn't say a word but I saw that he liked the food. Papa, I am so ashamed of how I behaved. I know it wasn't your fault we had to go. I am sorry. I always make things worse. Like not giving our proper name.

My eyelids are drooping now. There is still space below for Femi to add something in the morning. Please write to us.

Your loving daughter,
Sade

8 December 1995

My dear Femi and Sade,

I was so happy to hear your voices on the telephone last night. Even the few words you said to me, my dear son, Femi, they mean a lot to me. I long to hear more about how you are both getting on in your new schools. Perhaps, Femi, you will write like your sister?

I was very happy to receive your letter, Sade. You must not feel ashamed. It is only natural that you wanted us to stay together. Do not blame yourself for pretending your name was Adewale. It was, after all, Mama's family name. Lying is not in your nature. Mama and I always brought you up to respect the truth. But you have both been thrown into a situation that has forced you to act secretly. Remember that it was your Uncle Tunde and I who sent you out of the country. No child should have to go through what you two have. But the dishonesty and rottenness of those who have power in our country have now gone very deep. You know how much I hate cheating and doing things underhand. Yet I myself used another man's passport.

Mr. Nathan came today. He is cautious (just like your Uncle Tunde) but he is also hopeful that the British Home Office will give me Temporary Admission when they realize we are one family. He is going to ask them to treat the matter urgently. After that he will help me apply for political asylum so that we can stay here longer. I have made friends in here with a teacher from Somalia and am learning a lot from him. He says asylum applications are hard and we shall have to be patient. Zoka who comes from Bosnia told us their saying "Patience can break through iron doors." Your mama would have liked that. She would be pleased that I am also learning to be patient! It will be so much easier when we are together and we can help each other. As soon as I am free, I shall also begin the search for your Uncle Dele. His disappearance troubles me greatly.

In the meantime, please take good care of yourselves and each other. I hope to speak to you over the weekend. Give my very good wishes to your kind new auntie and uncle, Mr. and Mrs. King, and also to Mrs. Appiah. Write soon!

Your very loving Papa

P.S. I am drafting a letter to the Union of Journalists about the current situation for writers in Nigeria. They all know about Ken Saro-Wiwa but there are many others. I hope they will also support my application for asylum.

Avon School Library,
Monday 11 December

Dear Papa,

It is dinnertime and you can see I have come to the library. It is quiet in here and I like it. Your letter is in my coat pocket. I think there are good secrets and bad secrets. Your letter is a good one inside my pocket. Even Femi changed his mood a little when he read it this morning. Aunt Gracie says when they let you go, you can sleep in the sitting room here until you can sort things out. Uncle Roy follows the news about Nigeria and says it will be an honor to have you in their home!

You would have liked our English lesson this morning, Papa. We watched a TV program called *Making News*. It is about what is happening around the world. Did you know there is going to be a sports boycott of Nigeria by some European countries? They are protesting against the hanging of Mr. Saro-Wiwa and the other Ogoni leaders. The chief presenter is the same man on the Seven O'Clock News every night. But the other presenter is a child and she has to do real interviews. She only looked about my age. I would love to do that but I would be too nervous!

The work here at school is not a problem. In fact some of it is easier than at home, especially English! That surprised me. Most of the teachers are not so strict and some of the students are quite cheeky. I think they don't learn very much about Africa here. Some even think Africa is just one country and one boy asked me if I speak African! In Lower Primary, Mr. Obiki made us learn the names of all the different countries and languages in Europe. Do you remember how scared I was of Mr. Obiki? When his right eyebrow shot up like a question mark, that meant big trouble! I am glad he wasn't teaching me math this morning. His detective eyes would have seen my mind escaping from the classroom.

I am happy that you have some friends in prison like the teacher from Somalia. I am praying Mr. Nathan will be successful for you, Papa. There is something I need to talk to you about very badly.

That is the bell now. *O dabo* until later!

7 o'clock

Papa, I cannot believe they have said NO.

Mr. Nathan rang Mama Appiah and she came to tell us. Why won't they believe us, Papa? WHY??? Aunt Gracie said we should ring you but there is no point. I will just be crying. It is better to be like Femi — like a little stone.

Midnight

Papa, I can't hide this from you any longer. I can't sleep until I tell you. Before Mama Appiah left she went into the kitchen with Aunt Gracie. I could tell they were going to talk about you. I know I was wrong to listen to a conversation not meant for me. I am becoming underhand, a sneaking kind of person. You and Mama never wanted me to be like that, but I can't help it any more. Mama Appiah said Mr. Nathan is worried now about a bigger reason why they won't let you out of prison. Is it true, Papa? Is it true that Nigerian Police want you FOR MAMA'S MURDER? Is it true they have asked British Police to send you home? HOW CAN THEY TELL SUCH A GREAT BIG LIE? If only Femi and I had told the truth about everything right at the beginning, then the people here would know this is a TERRIBLE DISGUSTING LIE.

Sade

CHAPTER 31

SADE'S PLAN

SINCE THEIR VISIT to the Detention Center, Sade had been holding on to Papa's four little words, "We must be patient." Yet there were so many things she desperately wanted to talk about with him. Talking about Mama would be the hardest of all. However, more immediately, she needed his advice about what to do about Mariam and, of course, Marcia. To her relief, Marcia and Donna had completely ignored her again since the trip to Daud's Store. Neither of them had asked her why she had been away from school for two days afterward. But Mariam was also keeping away, sitting on the other side of the class. She was sure Mariam knew. What made it worse was that she was guilty not only of theft. Mariam had thought she was a friend and had confided in her. She was guilty of betrayal. Not knowing what to say or do, Sade had been avoiding Mariam too. With Papa's unexpected arrival, she had managed to push all of that to the back of her mind.

However, with this latest news, once again everything was spinning wildly out of control. She had a vision of Papa being bundled on to a plane by the Eyes and the Fingers.

How would "We must be patient" help then? Who would even know what was happening to Papa apart from themselves? That would surely suit the Eyes and the Fingers.

Out of sight, out of mind.

That would suit the Brass Buttons too.

When eventually she fell asleep in the early hours of the morning, Sade had a dream that was quite different from those that had been troubling her before.

She is sitting in a large empty classroom, her eyes fixed on a television screen. The Seven O'Clock News man moves his lips, but the screen is silent. He is in a desert and his pale hair is windblown, dusted with fine dry red sand. Like that swept down from the Sahara by the harmattan. His eyes concentrate down on her, narrowing, straining to see through the haze. She can tell from the way he leans forward that he is talking about something serious. Suddenly a photograph flashes on to the screen. It is of a round-faced man with daring eyes, a broad handsome smile and a pipe with a curved stem. Mr. Saro-Wiwa! Other faces follow that she doesn't recognize. The camera switches to a studio. The red dust vanishes, but Mr. Seven O'Clock's eyes remain narrowed on Sade. Swiveling sideways, he lowers his gaze toward someone shorter at the desk beside him. She is startled to find herself staring at herself.

When Sade's alarm buzzed in the morning, her head felt heavy as if it wanted to pull her back into sleep. But an idea was already hazily trying to enter her mind. Gradually it became clearer and sharper, demanding that she think about it. By the time Aunt Gracie knocked on her door, calling that it was time to get up, the idea had turned into a plan.

When Sade came downstairs for breakfast, Aunt Gracie did not reveal anything of what Mama Appiah had told her the night before. Sade could tell that she was trying hard to be bright as she prepared their cereal and sandwiches. When the telephone rang, Sade guessed it was Papa. Would he also try to keep back the awful news?

Papa, however, spoke openly about the latest turn in events. Matters were too serious to hide from them. This trumped-up charge against him proved that the government had a hand in Mama's murder and they were trying to cover up their crime. There was no time to lose. Mr. Nathan would make an immediate appeal and write to the British Home Secretary, while Papa would send his letter to the Union of Journalists. Sade listened. Papa was talking the way he used to speak with Mama. Each time his newspaper had to tackle a new problem with the authorities, he would talk through their plans with Mama.

"If our strategy and tactics are right, we can hold out against them. They have the power, but we have intelligence!"

Now Mama was dead and Uncle Tunde was far away, whom could Papa talk to? So he was explaining to her, his daughter.

"I don't believe the British will send me back. Anyway, not so soon after the Saro-Wiwa affair." Papa's voice had been steady but now he hesitated.

"I don't want you and Femi to worry. Let me talk to Femi now."

Femi held the receiver like a wooden statue. Apart from tiny humming grunts, he didn't reply to Papa. Sade took the receiver back to say *o dabo*. Papa's voice had become very quiet.

Sade waited until she had closed the latch on the gate and was walking beside her brother. The bare trees along the pavement stretched upward like elderly hands with knuckled fingers, begging.

"I know a way to help Papa. Will you come with me after school?"

"Where?" Femi frowned at her suspiciously.

"I can't tell you yet. I have to check something first. Both of us must go," Sade declared calmly.

"What will Auntie say?"

"I'll ring her—after school. I'll tell her that we'll be late. This is very important, Femi."

"I'll miss my programs if I go."

Sade swung to a halt. She grabbed Femi's arm and made him face her.

"What's wrong with you? This is more important than watching TV! It's not playing. Don't you want to help Papa?" she demanded. A glimmer of hurt flickered in Femi's eyes before they shut themselves in again. He remained silent, his jaw set tight.

"Well, if you want to help, meet me at the bus stop opposite your school. I'll be there at three-thirty." Sade tugged sharply at her rucksack straps and marched ahead. Farther down the road, guilt began to niggle at her for leaving Femi like that. She needed him for her plan. But it was no use begging, or even prodding, him. He would simply retreat more into his shell. No, she just had to face him roughly with the choice. Either he helped Papa or he didn't. But even if he did not come, she would still have to carry it through, as best as she could, on her own.

At break, Sade hurried to the library. On previous days, she had watched the librarian help students who came with different questions. Mrs. Howe would point them to the right books or to the computer. Throughout the morning's lessons Sade had silently tried out various ways of asking her question. Everything depended on it. She might have asked her English teacher, but was worried that Mr. Morris would become curious and ask unwelcome questions. She was not yet ready for that. She was at the top of the stairs leading to the library, when she almost came face to face with Mariam. Sade turned aside so hastily, and pushed open the library door so forcefully, that she would not have been surprised if Mrs. Howe had sent her right back out. The librarian flared with annoyance, ready to order the noise vandal out. But as she met Sade's eyes, her anger strangely dropped.

"What is it?" she asked evenly.

"Excuse me," Sade's voice fell to a whisper. "I need the address for the Seven O'Clock News—the television studio—please."

Fifteen minutes later, Sade eased her way through students crowding the stairs and corridors with the address on a piece of paper in her pocket. It was somewhere near the center of London, according to Mrs. Howe. At lunchtime, Sade returned to the library to study a map. On the back of the paper with the address, she drew a rough map and wrote in the names of roads and places that she would need to recognize. She would ask at the bus stop which was the right bus. She and Femi had managed it once before all on their own. It should be easier now, she told herself. Nor was she worried about the fares, having saved most of her pocket money from Aunt Gracie. Her biggest worry was Femi. She fervently hoped that he would come with her. She needed him for her plan as much as she needed his company.

Sade reached the bus shelter at half-past three and scanned the small group of waiting passengers. No Femi huddling among them. Only a couple of children were still waiting outside Greenslades School. They wound their arms around their coats to keep out the wind whipping down the street. Femi must have gone back to his television programs. Aunt Gracie would have a piece of cake and a drink waiting for him and the house would be warm. She couldn't blame him. She should have explained more of her plan to him instead of being so secretive. But she had told him it was for Papa. Didn't he care?

Sade looked for a notice about the buses. A small board, with the glass broken, indicated the place where there had once been information about bus numbers and routes. Her eyes trailed across to Femi's school again. The two children had gone and the school looked deserted. If she was already feeling cold and lonely, it was going to be far worse later this evening. She was wondering whom to ask about the bus when someone tugged her coat. She swung around. Femi had come after all! She could have hugged him. Instead she grinned.

"Where we are going?" he asked solemnly.

CHAPTER 32

MR. SEVEN O'CLOCK NEWS

"DON'T WORRY, AUNTIE. We'll be all right." Sade tried to sound confident. Femi trickled his fingers down the misty glass of the cramped phone booth. The concern in Aunt Gracie's voice sparked through the telephone wires. It was going to be a freezing night. They could get lost. London was dangerous. Their father would be terribly worried if he knew. Why did they have to go on their own? Uncle could take them. He would come for them if they would just say where they were now and where they wanted to go. Three pips called urgently for more coins.

"Please, Auntie. We'll come—"

The line went dead. Sade's hand trembled as she replaced the receiver. How could she explain that this was something she and Femi had to do by themselves? So many dreadful, frightening things happened to people that were never reported. Like to Mariam's family. Or to those people at the Screening Unit—like the mother with the face of sunken dunes. With so many stories, why should Papa's tale matter enough to become news? But if Mr. Seven O'Clock saw two children on their own, he might just stop to listen. It was up to her and Femi to show that it mattered.

They jumped on the first bus with Waterloo Bridge on its list of destinations. It was one of the names Sade had written on her own map. She would have liked to ask the driver where the bus would go after that. But he was a scowling man who shoved back their change so roughly that she kept quiet. The bus downstairs was full of passengers. Femi clumped up the stairs and Sade followed him without protest. It would also be easier to see from on top.

"We have to look out for the river," she told Femi, without adding that it was her only sure landmark.

The bus carried them over the Thames. On either side, along the riverbank, great buildings towered like castles with thousands of lights sparkling between the violet sky and the mud-colored water. The river looked nothing like the fat bright blue snake on the library map crossed by a zigzag of yellow stripes. It seemed even more remote from the squiggle of lines on the map in her hand. On the library map, she had counted five big yellow streets that they would have to cross before the long road where they would find the television studio. But there had been lots of little streets between the yellow ones and Sade was soon confused. Every street outside the bus appeared large enough to be colored yellow! She had to do something quickly before the bus moved too far from the river and she lost her bearings altogether.

"Excuse me, can you tell us where we are on this map, please? We want to go here, please." Swallowing her shyness, Sade propelled her sketch toward a young man sitting alongside them. He blinked in surprise, then brought the paper so close to his face that it almost touched his nose. The longer he spent examining it, the faster Sade felt her heart pumping. Her map was much too rough! She should have copied it out more clearly. By the time the man could make sense of it, they would have gone too far. They should at least get off the bus. She was poising herself to speak when the young man handed the map back. They were in luck. The bus would actually go along the end of the road they were looking for, he said. He would point it out to them.

Once off the bus, the children steered their way through figures wrapped securely in coats and scarves. Shops and offices were closing and people were going home. A plump Father Christmas and an airy snowman twinkled down at them above the street lights. Giant stars and Christmas trees flickered above the traffic. However, around the corner, the road was not lit so brightly. Cars and taxis still roared past, but there were fewer shops and people. More shadows.

"Listen, child. London streets are full of strangers—and some are very sick, you know. Your daddy is trusting me and Uncle Roy to take good care of you."

Aunt Gracie's words echoed in Sade's head. She remembered Darth Vader of the alley lunging out at them on their first night in the city.

"How far is it?" Femi mewled. Sade was peering through the gloom at each new entrance, searching for signs and brass number plates. She had no idea what kind of building they were looking for.

"It can't be far."

"You lie! How do you know? You haven't been here

before!" It was the whine that always got on her nerves.

"Then why ask me such a stupid question?!" Sade bit her lip. The moment the words were out she knew that they were a mistake. Femi stamped to a halt.

"If I'm so stupid, why do you need me? I'm going home! Give me my bus money!"

"Don't be so—" Sade swung around. Femi's jaw jutted out fiercely. He was serious. He might even try to walk all the way if she refused to give him his bus fare. Her whole plan was going to be ruined.

"Oh don't let's argue!" Sade pleaded. "I'm sorry. It's me that's stupid. We won't help Papa if we fight."

Slowly Femi's jaw and shoulders relaxed. Like a bristling cat letting its hair down. They set off again in silence. Ahead of them most of the buildings were shrouded in darkness. Was this really the right street? Sade would have liked to check her map under one of the pools of light but she dare not let Femi see any doubt. Her face prickled with the cold and her fingers stiffened despite her gloves.

A glow of light and two taxis pulling up alongside a row of great white pillars were the first signs. When they drew nearer, they could see the building was quite different from the rest. Behind the pillars, the pavement sloped up toward two large revolving glass doors. The entire wall was made of glass. Inside a brilliantly lit hall, glossy green trees grew in huge tubs and televisions hung from the walls like decorations. For a little while they stared without speaking at this world inside a world. They could see everything but hear nothing. People walked briskly from the revolving doors to a man behind a desk. The buttons on his uniform glinted as he nodded and pointed.

"Will that man let us in?" Femi asked.

Sade had only imagined being with Mr. Seven O'Clock himself. She hadn't thought about getting past any guards! And if she had to ask for him, what would she say? Suddenly she couldn't even remember his real name! Whatever would she call him? Hardly 'Mr. Seven O'Clock News'!

"We'll have to wait outside. No one can chase us away from here." Sade tried to keep her voice low and calm. Mr. Seven O'Clock was probably inside the studio already. At Papa's office, the journalists worked for hours before the paper was published each day. She and Femi might have to wait until the program was over. She raised her watch toward the light inside the glass wall. Just past five-thirty. The news finished at eight. She hadn't thought about the waiting time.

"You're mad! It's free-eezing!" Femi dug his hands deeper into his pockets.

"When he sees that we waited in the cold, he'll listen to us!" insisted Sade.

"We might be dead!"

"Be serious, Femi. You know what I mean."

"I am serious! You are the one with crazy ideas!" Femi's voice rose indignantly. He blew out a mouthful of air and a thin mist of steam rose under the lamplight.

"Like Papa," he added under his breath.

Sade was not sure she had heard correctly. She did not want another argument. Certainly not one about Papa—nor outside the television studio. It was unlikely that Mr. Seven

O'Clock would appear before eight. Femi was probably right. They would freeze just standing there.

"OK, we'll come back later. I've got money. We'll get fish and chips. I know you like them." Before he could push her away, Sade put her arm around Femi and steered him once again into the shadows.

As soon as she had said fish and chips, Sade wished she hadn't. They had not passed any fish and chips shops along the way. They would have to walk farther on up the road, which seemed even darker than the direction from which they had come.

"We can go there!" Femi pointed to a restaurant on the other side of the road.

For a brief moment, it seemed ideal. If they sat near the front window, they could keep an eye on the entrance to the television studio. But even before they had stepped on to the pavement, Sade knew it was not possible. Silver cutlery glinted off linen tablecloths. A waiter was folding napkins and placing them upright like fox ears. Another was beginning to light candles.

"We don't have enough money for this place, Femi."

"Let me see," he said boldly. There was a menu by the door. "What does this mean, Sade?" Suddenly there was an edge of caution in his voice. Some words were in French but before Sade could reply, Femi whistled.

"Fourteen pounds!"

Femi pointed to an item about fish baked in wine with ingredients Sade had never heard of. She pulled at Femi's arm. This time he did not resist.

The farther they walked from the television studio, the more murky and desolate the street became. There was something menacing and grim about the buildings as if phantoms might be lurking behind the doors. She tried not to let Femi feel her fear. However when three figures emerged in the dimness ahead and came reeling toward them, she clutched her brother's arm. He, in turn, snatched her away toward the road. They hovered on the edge of the gutter, for a moment trapped between the staggering bodies and the headlights of a vehicle. Then a strong stench of alcohol hit them and a sound like a bull in pain. As the car's rearlights receded like discs of fire, they dashed across the road. Sade was about to urge that they should turn back, when Femi pointed to a light shining from a doorway in the next block. They would go as far as that.

It was a tiny shop and the shopkeeper was bringing out a grille to close for the night. The children slipped inside behind him. The man's cap and tunic reminded Sade of Mariam's uncle, although Daud's Store was twice the size. But here too, newspapers, magazines, sweets, biscuits, drinks and all sorts were crammed on to narrow shelves. Certainly no fish and chips. Sade grabbed a packet of chocolate biscuits and Femi yanked open the cabinet with canned drinks. The man studied them with a weary patience as Sade handed him her coins.

Femi did not argue as they set off back toward the television studio. Nor did he mention fish and chips again. Ahead of them the great white pillars now stood out like distant beacons. Once again, the revolving doors and the lights both beckoned them and held them at bay. Sade was painfully aware of the time. Two more hours outside in the cold. The only place that seemed to offer any shelter was a small recess next to the restaurant with the silver cutlery and candles. It was actually a doorway set back from the road and at first Sade expected someone to come out at any minute. If they were asked what they were doing, she would say that they were waiting for their father and then move away. Where to, she did not know.

Femi tore open the packet of chocolate biscuits. Two biscuits were enough for Sade but Femi continued munching until only a couple were left. Sade decided not to drink her Coke. It would make her even colder, but Femi ignored her advice and gulped the contents of his can. After he had finished, he stood with his teeth chattering. Sade suggested they play word games to pass the time, but Femi was not interested. For a while she tried running on the spot to keep warm, but felt her legs becoming so heavy with the cold that it was too much effort to move. Femi was now frozen into silence and did not resist when Sade pressed close to him, twining her arm through his. At least they could share whatever little body heat they had together.

All the while, Sade kept her eyes trained on the other side of the road. The revolving doors were never still for long. It was like watching a strange dance inside and outside the glass. Some people stepped away purposefully, but very often a figure strode onto the pavement with an arm held aloft as if raising a flag. A black taxi would roll up, absorb the figure and whisk it away. Sometimes the arm had to swoop up and down a number of times before a vehicle came. Only occasionally did someone cross the street as if coming toward them. But no one appeared to notice the children.

It was difficult to see her watch in their dark corner. Sade made herself wait a little longer each time before trying to check it, as if that might hurry the minutes along. Instead the long needle seemed to become slower and stiffer. When at last it was ten minutes to eight, she and Femi had become just as stiff themselves. They hobbled across the road together and placed themselves alongside the glass wall a little way aside from the revolving doors. It was still better not to attract the attention of Mr. Buttons behind the desk.

Eight o'clock. Five past. Where was Mr. Seven O'Clock? Quarter past. Was it possible to become paralyzed through cold? Twenty past. A tall thin man with silver-gray hair who had his back turned to them was walking away with one arm raised. Surely that was him! How had they missed him coming through the door? He was calling a taxi! He would be gone before he had seen them. Sade wrenched Femi from the glass wall and tried to run. Her bones felt brittle enough to snap.

"Please! Wait! Please!" her words fluttered out jerkily. Mr. Seven O'Clock turned as Femi slipped, slid and tumbled toward his feet. Swinging an arm forward, Mr. Seven O'Clock grasped him just before he hit the ground. A black taxi purred to a halt next to them.

"Please . . . please!" Sade's words were as cracked as her lips. "We need . . . to see you . . . please!"

Mr. Seven O'Clock's eyes were larger than she had

imagined. His forehead furrowed as he helped Femi up. Then glancing across at the taxi driver, he shook his head. Sade's heart leaped. He was going to listen after all.

"You had better come inside. It looks as if you could do with a hot drink first."

Guided through the glass doors, past the desk and Mr. Buttons, into the lift and through corridors, Sade ignored the curious eyes, aware only of the tall man behind them. He was like a great sail, pushing them forward. Protecting them.

Outside, Sade had tried to rehearse where to begin. From the shot that killed Mama? Or before that, with Papa's articles? Or later, with Papa and the false passport? There were so many possible starting points. In the end she did not need to worry. Mr. Seven O'Clock waited patiently as he sat opposite the two children. With a sense of touch beginning to flow back into her fingers around the mug of hot chocolate on the table in front of her, Sade found the thread she needed.

She began with Papa, locked up in Heathlands Detention Center. Papa who believed so strongly in telling the truth that his articles made the Brass Button Generals in their home country very angry. So angry that gunmen had tried to kill him and killed Mama instead . . . Slowly she unraveled the tale. Mr. Seven O'Clock's nods encouraged her. Finally she explained that the Immigration people were thinking about sending Papa back into the arms of those who wanted to do away with Papa. They did not seem to understand. That was why she and Femi had come here. Mr. Seven O'Clock leaned forward.

"And what about you two? You haven't said much about

yourselves. Where do you go to school?" he probed gently.

Despite the soft tread of his words, they disturbed something deep inside Sade. Like a buried mine erupting. The wall behind Mr. Seven O'Clock faded and she saw him as he had been in her dream with his keen blue eyes straining against the sun and the dust-filled wind. She couldn't take them looking into her anymore. They would surely see what kind of person she had become. Tears swamped her. Embarrassed, she tried to wipe them away. She had not prepared herself to talk about themselves.

"I am sorry. I didn't mean—" Mr. Seven O'Clock delved into his coat pocket and pulled out a neatly pressed handkerchief to hand to Sade.

"We were smuggled." Femi arched his eyebrows. He had been stubbornly silent until now, not saying a word. Sade had even had to give his name to Mr. Seven O'Clock. But now—just when she suddenly felt herself falling apart—Femi was stepping in to rescue her.

"It was horrible," he announced.

He spoke bluntly about Mrs. Bankole. How she had taken Uncle Tunde's money to pretend that they were her children, then deserted them as soon as they arrived in England. How they had been left all alone because they could not find their Uncle Dele. How a man in a dark alley robbed them and how a man in a video shop had accused them of being thieves! And Femi told Mr. Seven O'Clock how they had themselves been fingerprinted in the Asylum Screening Unit—just as if they *were* thieves.

More words flowed from Femi than he had uttered in

weeks. His outspoken words made him sound almost like Papa! Then, as suddenly as he began, he stopped. He seemed to have exhausted himself. Mr. Seven O'Clock's face was grave. Who was taking care of them now, he asked, and where were they living? He would arrange a taxi to take them back. He thanked them for coming and for telling him their story. Certainly he would look into Papa's case further. However, he could not promise it would be made into a news item. Shepherded once again through the corridors, past doors behind which journalists prepared the news, Sade felt her heart quietly throb.

CHAPTER 33

WAITING

THE TAXI ENGINE CHUGGED noisily while the children clambered out. The front door swung open. Even from the gate Sade could see the worry in Aunt Gracie's face. The gray in her hair seemed to have streaked her cheeks. Uncle Roy had his arm around her. He looked solemn rather than cross. Aunt Gracie quietly insisted that the children eat before Sade was asked to explain exactly where they had been and what they had done. Femi was silent again. When Sade spoke, she fixed her gaze on Aunt Gracie's collar. It was her fault that Aunt Gracie had been so upset and that Uncle Roy had been out searching the streets for them. But as she related how Mr. Seven O'Clock had given them hot chocolate and how he had listened so carefully, both adults seemed to ease a little.

"So he really listened to your story?" Aunt Gracie asked.

"He looks a decent enough man. Now we must wait and see, nuh?" Uncle Roy was cautious.

The following evening at seven o'clock the children joined Aunt Gracie and Uncle Roy in front of the television. The main stories always came first, then the rest of the news. Sade had made a special telephone call to Papa to make sure that he too was watching, but she avoided telling him exactly how she and Femi had got to see Mr. Seven O'Clock. Papa had sounded pleased. All the detainees shared a single television. Most of them eagerly followed the news just like Papa, always hoping to hear something from their own countries. A few preferred the game shows, films or sports, and arguments occasionally flared up. But Papa had been confident that he could persuade the others tonight. Sade tried to imagine them. Papa trying to remain calm, perhaps with his friends from Somalia and Bosnia next to him. Would they really believe that Papa's children could get his story on to television?

That night, Mr. Seven O'Clock and the other presenters said nothing at all about Papa. Nor the evening after.

"Don't give up yet," Uncle Roy advised. "They have to check everything. It must take time getting the information from Nigeria."

But Sade's hopes were dipping. On the telephone, Papa was sounding quieter. No letter had come back yet from the Union of Journalists and there was no further news from Mr. Nathan. She could not concentrate in any of her classes. Even in English, where Mr. Morris asked them to research and write a short piece for a news program such as *Making News*. They had to work in pairs and Mr. Morris had put her with Mariam. Their silences were awkward. Especially when Donna poked her head between them.

"What's up then? I thought you were mates and all!"

Sade would have liked to slap the grin from her face. But instead Donna's words burned into her. Mariam looked miserable as well. Both Sade and Mariam told each other that they had no ideas for a news program.

On Friday evening after supper, Sade said she was going to her bedroom to do her homework. Instead she crept under her quilt, staying there until just before seven when she forced herself downstairs. Auntie and Uncle were watching the television, but Femi had turned his back. He was slapping cards on to the carpet in a game of patience, making clicking and sucking sounds with his tongue and teeth. Sade sank into the sofa. Mr. Seven O'Clock was behind his desk waiting for the fanfare of music to stop. If nothing else, she liked his tie. It was pleasantly bright—pawpaw orange shading into a sunset of red, pink and purple. Papa disliked wearing ties, but even he might like this one. They hadn't spoken for a couple of days. Was he still bothering to get people to watch this news?

Suddenly Sade sat bolt upright. Papa was smiling from a large square behind Mr. Seven O'Clock! A much younger Papa, but definitely their father!

"Femi! Look!"

Femi swiveled around.

"A Nigerian journalist, Mr. Folarin Solaja, currently being detained after attempting to enter Britain illegally, is at the center of a growing dispute. A spokesman for the Nigerian government has said that Mr. Solaja is wanted for murder and should be returned to Nigeria. Mr. Solaja, however, is claiming political asylum. Coming so soon after the execution of the Nigerian writer Mr. Ken Saro-Wiwa, the case is politically sensitive. Mr. Nelson Mandela, president of South Africa, has continued to urge a tougher line against Nigeria's military dictators. But here in Britain the government has been taking a tougher line against asylum seekers, claiming that many are not genuine refugees. To discuss the situation, we have in the studio Tara Mosam, a writer and filmmaker, who has recently returned from Nigeria, where she followed the case of Ken Saro-Wiwa. Tara Mosam, first of all, what do you know of Folarin Solaja?"

The camera swung to an earnest young woman with a bob of black hair fanning out from her cheeks.

"Folarin Solaja is well known within Nigeria as one of a small band of very courageous journalists who still dares to tell the truth about abuses of human rights by the military government. He writes for the small but important weekly paper *Speak,* which has been playing a dangerous cat-and-mouse game with the authorities. The newspaper's staff have moved their offices several times to avoid being closed down by the police. But unlike Ken Saro-Wiwa, Mr. Solaja is not well known outside Nigeria."

"What events actually led him to seek asylum here?" Mr. Seven O'Clock leaned slightly forward like he had done across the table a few nights earlier.

"About five weeks ago there was an attempt on his life. Unknown gunmen called at his house, fatally shooting his wife instead of him. Apparently he had been receiving death threats for some time but had ignored them. However, after the assassination of his wife, he went into hiding. The Home Office says that he was arrested a couple of weeks ago trying to enter through London Airport on a false passport. They say that he did not declare on arrival that he was a political refugee and that he did not ask for political asylum until his identity was challenged. So they intend to deport him."

"Is there anything stopping them?"

"Mr. Solaja has appealed on the grounds that his life will be in danger if he is returned to Nigeria and also that his children are here in England. He says they were smuggled here immediately after their mother's death. But the Home Office claims to have no record of them."

Mr. Seven O'Clock looked grave. Was he going to say that he had actually met them? Tell everyone watching that the Home Office was wrong. Sade felt blood flush to her face.

"I gather that there is a warrant out for Mr. Solaja's arrest in Nigeria." Mr. Seven O'Clock was straightening up.

"Yes, a further twist. Mr. Solaja has now been accused of murdering his wife and Nigeria wants him extradited. Already some Nigerians are saying that the murder charge is an attempt to throw a cloak over the real assassins. But of course it would be extremely dangerous for Folarin Solaja if he were to be deported. As you know there was a great deal of criticism about the trial of Ken Saro-Wiwa and his colleagues."

"Well, I imagine we shall be hearing more of this case. Thank you very much, Tara Mosam. After the break we shall—"

Uncle Roy began to clap.

"Congratulations, children! My goodness! You actually did it!"

"But he didn't say it was us—that we told him!" Femi looked confused.

"Our English teacher says you have to stick to the main points," explained Sade.

"That was probably it," Aunt Gracie said gently. "But now that your daddy is in the news, it won't be so easy for them to send him straight back!"

In the morning, Uncle Roy took Sade and Femi to the library to search through the day's newspapers. Three of them had printed stories about Papa, one with the same photograph of Papa as a young man. On the way home they stopped to buy their own copies. They spread the newspapers out on the dining-room table to read them again. Suddenly Sade spotted a couple of sentences near the end of one report that they had all missed before: *A spokesperson for Nigerians for Democracy announced that his organization would mount a demonstration on Sunday for the release of Mr. Solaja. Unconfirmed reports suggest that Mr. Solaja has begun a hunger strike in protest at his detention.*

CHAPTER 34

OUT OF THE SHADOWS

A SMALL CONGREGATION of faces and placards greeted them as the children and Uncle Roy walked toward the high wire fence at Heathlands Detention Center. Sade scanned the messages: SOLAJA MUST STAY! REMEMBER KEN SARO-WIWA! NIGERIA NEEDS A FREE PRESS! NO MORE DEPORTATIONS! GIVE REFUGEES A FAIR DEAL! The people looked friendly, talking, laughing, calling out. All because of Papa! This would cheer him. The children had spoken to him after seeing the television news and the newspapers. Sade had asked if it was true about the hunger strike. Papa had replied that they must not worry. The most important thing was for his case to be public. But every time Sade ate, she thought of Papa. What was it like not to eat at all?

Behind the wire, a guard crossed the courtyard, his head erect, ignoring the crowd. But from high above the cameras pointed down in their direction and when Sade glanced ahead to her right, she received a shock. Three police vans, full of black uniforms behind the windows, were waiting in the car park near the gate. Were they really expecting trouble?

"Uncle, why—" Before she finished, shouting broke out.

"Solaja must stay!"

"No deportation!"

A policeman and woman marched calmly out of the gate toward the vans.

"Solaja must stay! No deportation!"

Uncle Roy tightened his grip on Sade's hand. Femi edged a little closer to his sister as they approached the gate and the demonstrators.

A man in the crowd stepped out and addressed Uncle Roy.

"Sir, are these, by any chance, Solaja's children? The boy looks just like him." He spoke with a strong Nigerian accent.

Femi frowned but looked pleased at the same time.

"They are," replied Uncle Roy.

"Listen, good people!" called the man, waving a cloth cap. "This fine young boy and girl are Folarin Solaja's children. The ones the Immigration say don't exist! But here they are coming to see their own daddy!"

All around them people started to clap.

"Please tell him we support him all the way," the man continued enthusiastically. "Tell him that we like what he writes. Nigeria needs more brave people like him."

The children and Uncle Roy smiled.

"Tell him we won't give up. We shall demonstrate for him until they let him go! You know—"

"*You* better let *them* go now, Deji!" interrupted another man. He laughed. "They didn't come to hear one of your big speeches!"

"Oh sorry, sorry," Mr. Big Speech apologized. "But we

want your daddy to know he has many friends."

Mr. Big Speech reminded Sade of Mr. Abiona who kept the stall down their road. He was such a fan of Papa's that he had often praised him when the children came to buy anything.

"Thank you, sir," she said. "We'll tell Papa."

The gate that had curiously swung open for them on their previous visit with Mama Appiah remained closed this time until they were actually standing in front of it. They searched for a bell to ring for entry. Sade could see the Eyes behind the plate glass in the security office inspecting them. Then the buzzer sounded and the gate unlocked. Inside the office, the guards were grimly silent. The calls and shouts of the demonstrators were muffled from here. When Uncle Roy announced that they had come to see Mr. Solaja, even the air seemed to stiffen.

They followed a guard across the open yard to the next locked gate. The demonstrators on the other side of the fence waved and yelled messages of support. Giving a little wave back, Sade felt embarrassed. She was cheating. They would not wave if they knew how she had behaved to Mariam and her family. If only she could talk to Papa now about what she should do. But Papa had far too many bigger problems to worry about.

"He's in there already." The woman guard had a face like a china doll's. Her green eyes signed toward the visitors' room. Who else was there to see Papa? Sade and Femi darted ahead of Uncle Roy. Papa was sitting in the far corner, facing the door. The visitor's back was turned to them but when he twisted around, Sade gasped. Uncle Dele! He looked a lot older than Sade remembered. A tumult of words and hugs followed. Papa pulled Uncle Roy into the circle, shaking his hand and thanking him many times over.

"Well, well! My little Olufemi! Folasade! Both so grown up!" Uncle Dele's eyes looked a little moist as they settled into a huddle of chairs.

"Your beard is like Papa's! You also copied Uncle Tunde!" Femi sniggered.

"We couldn't find you! Where have you been, Uncle Dele?" Sade was almost accusing.

"It's a long story and this beard even comes into it!" Uncle Dele laughed lightly, scratching the trim black border.

"After what these children have been through, it won't come as a surprise," Papa sighed.

In his spare time Uncle Dele had been working with Nigerians for Democracy in London. They had been arguing that Nigeria should not be allowed to attend the Commonwealth Conference. In fact, they wanted Nigeria to be expelled from the Commonwealth until there were proper elections that allowed people to vote freely for a new government. Then the threats had started, over the telephone, both at home and at the Art College. At first their uncle had ignored them, but then they grew menacing. The day after Ken Saro-Wiwa was hanged, a note was slipped through the letterbox at his flat. It said "You Next." He had gone into hiding immediately.

"That was just two days before Mama was shot," Papa added quietly.

Some English friends had given Uncle Dele a safe place

to stay in the countryside for a few weeks. He had not been able to read any Nigerian newspapers and had been cut off from all his usual contacts for the last few weeks. At least one of them must be a spy. The Seven O'Clock News on Friday night had been a terrible shock for him. He had to come out of hiding to help Papa. In fact the press were coming this evening to interview him outside the Detention Center.

"But . . . this hunger strike of yours, Folarin." Uncle Dele lowered his voice. "I don't think that it's a good idea. Think of your health. Please."

"My brother, what else can I do?" Papa threw up his hands. His face looked thinner than before. "A hunger strike makes news. It *stays* news. OK, not for too long, but people will want to know what's happening. These Immigration people can't steal me away on a plane when others are watching them."

Sade watched Papa's fingers at their gymnastics. Uncle Tunde had often tried to get their father to change his mind, but once Papa had worked out his reasons, it was like trying to uproot a baobab tree. She had always loved to hear Papa argue. He said things in ways that always made matters sharper. How she wished she could talk to him about Mariam. Alone.

They had already hugged Papa good-bye when he hastily pulled an envelope from his pocket.

"Nearly forgot! For Master and Miss Solaja, personal delivery!" Papa made a small mock bow. Sade took the letter.

"Keep writing, my child," Papa added softly. "As long as we have our pens, we can talk."

Papa's words swirled in Sade's mind as the wooden door crashed heavily behind them. The children, Uncle Roy and Uncle Dele trailed behind the guard in silence across the pools of yellow that lit up the two prison yards. Outside the final gate, they were greeted by cheers and a flash of camera lights.

CHAPTER 35

DARE TO TELL

My dear children,

When you were little, your Mama and I used to tell you stories. So did your grandparents, Uncle Tunde, Mama Buki – in fact many of us elders who loved you dearly. I am sure you will remember Tortoise. He might have been slow like a bent old man, but was he not always quick-witted? Sometimes he was artful and cunning, sometimes sensible and wise! There is one story I especially want to tell you now. It is one in which Tortoise is all these things as well as being courageous and daring. Perhaps you have heard it before. Never mind. The beauty is that we usually do not tire of hearing these stories again. What makes this one extra special is that it is also a story about stories!

LEOPARD AND TORTOISE

Once upon a time, a hungry leopard was searching for something to eat. He had been prowling around all day without any luck. His stomach was beginning to feel pinched. As evening drew in, he came to a clearing in the forest—and there, in front of him, was a Tortoise. In one single swoop, Leopard slapped down his paw on Tortoise's back.

"Oh please," cried Tortoise. "I can see this is truly my end. But please, Mighty Leopard, just grant me a few minutes' grace before you devour me. I wish to prepare myself to leave this world." Now Leopard knew that Tortoise could not escape. He also thought that a little time would allow his stomach juices to prepare to receive Tortoise!

"As I am in a good mood," he growled. "I'll give you five minutes."

As soon as Leopard released him, Tortoise began to scratch furiously at the grass under his feet. He worked in ever-increasing circles. He hardly stopped to breathe. Leopard watched, amazed. Whatever was Tortoise doing?

When Tortoise had used up every last second, he looked around at the deep marks that he had etched into the earth around him.

"Tell me," said Leopard. "Why have you done this?"

"Well," replied Tortoise. "From now on, anyone who comes to this place will see that some creature put up a great struggle for life here. You may eat me, but it is my struggle that shall be remembered!"

My dear children, do not worry. I do not intend to be eaten up by any Leopard! But like Tortoise, I believe in the power of the stories we tell. If we keep quiet about injustice, then injustice wins. We must dare to tell. Across the oceans of time, words are mightier than swords.

Your loving Papa

CHAPTER 36

SORRY

MIST WRAPPED ITSELF around the school. It threaded through the skeleton trees that lined the driveway and clung to the frostbitten bushes opposite them.

Very early in the morning, there is sometimes mist in the forest. It lifts in waves like a long-tailed bird forced into the open. Forced to reveal the nest it wanted to hide. Scents of forest and damp earth rise up with the mist. Grandma never allows them out of the compound until the mist has gone. She tells stories of people who lose their way because of it. Stories of iwin, *the tree sprites who play wild games and make the wanderers scramble out of the woods with eyes flickering and madness on their tongues.*

Sade peered through the gloom ahead. She recognized the slim figure walking alone with her head bent forward, covered by a scarf. She hurried to catch up with Mariam.

"Please. Can we go somewhere? There's something I need to tell you," Sade whispered. Her heart pounded.

• • •

The hall was hardly private. If Marcia and Donna were there, Sade did not want to see them. However the noisy batches of students took no notice of them as they weaved their way toward an unoccupied corner. Mariam turned to Sade with folded arms. Her dark eyes waited, silently on guard.

"I stole from your uncle's shop—a lighter, a cigarette lighter." Sade watched for horror and disgust to change the silent face. But not a muscle seemed to move. Mariam's gaze remained steady. As steadfast as Mama's eyes would have been.

"Marcia said her cousin would hurt my brother." Sade forced herself to continue. "She and Donna came with me. I took the lighter while they kept talking to your uncle and—" Sade hesitated. Her heart was flapping wildly. "That lady is your mother, isn't she?"

Mariam nodded and Sade watched the navy blue head scarf ripple slightly. She recalled how the thin bony-faced woman in Daud's Store had also stared at her in this guarded way.

"My mother, my uncle, they know about the lighter."

Mariam's voice was so soft and flat that Sade was unsure she had heard correctly.

"Marcia and Donna, they do the same to me," Mariam continued evenly. "But you stop talking with me. Like you don't want to be my friend," Mariam accused her quietly.

"They . . . you . . . all know? Why didn't your uncle stop me? What did Marcia do to you?" Sade's tongue felt dry and clumsy as her questions stumbled over each other. She ignored the shrill ringing over the tannoy.

215

"They make me steal. From Uncle. I must give them gold pen or they do something bad. Like fire! But I tell Mama and Uncle and he give me the pen. He say, 'Let them think you steal it. People like that are no good. Don't fight them. Just keep away.' I give Marcia the pen and they leave me alone. But now I see them start with you."

Sade did not know what to say or where to look. So Mariam and her family had known all along! Papa would surely not have said the same as Mariam's uncle. How did people know what was the right thing to do? It was all so confusing. Yet she admired Mariam for telling her mother and uncle. At least they had all faced the threats together.

The hall was almost empty. Sade forced herself to look straight into Mariam's face. The bell was ringing again.

"I'm sorry," she said. "You told me all about your uncle and your mother." Mariam had even spoken about her father's death in prison and her brother who was missing. "I told you nothing."

Mariam's eyes seemed to soften.

"It's OK. Maybe you worried about something," she said. "Come. Morrissy go mad if we late. You see me at break?"

Mr. Morris was calling the register when they entered the class. Sade expected him to say something cross or sarcastic. However, his gaze seemed to rest on her for an extra second like he was taking a snapshot on slow shutter speed. He simply said, "Ah, there you are!" Marcia's narrowing eyes could not hide a flicker of surprise as Sade followed Mariam down the aisle. Was it at seeing them together again?

"Why don't you tell them off, sir? You tell us off if we come late!" Donna's words were as spiky as her hair.

"Indeed I would, Donna. If only to hear whether your latest excuse was any better than your last!" Mr. Morris's words produced muffled laughter and giggles. There even seemed to be some snorts from Kevin's desk.

At the end of the register, Mr. Morris announced that the class could talk quietly among themselves until the bell. Then he signaled to Sade.

"I'd like a word in private with you, Sade."

"Telling you off in private! That's discrimination, that is," Donna hissed into Sade's ear.

"Do you want me, sir? I come late with Sade." Mariam stood up with Sade. She was coming to her aid. Despite everything.

"*A friend in need*," Mama would say.

"No, thank you, Mariam. This concerns Sade only," said Mr. Morris. His eyes roamed the classroom. "I shall just be outside in the corridor. If your chattering lifts the ceiling, my Christmas present to you will be detention."

Sade followed Mr. Morris, feeling dull and numb. What now? Why did he have to notice her? She had more than enough to worry about already. In her other life, if a teacher wanted to have words with her, she would quickly think of Iyawo sitting quietly on her desk at home. Iyawo, who held up her graceful neck and lace-patterned head so calmly. That used to soothe any butterflies in her stomach. She tried to think of her Iyawo now. But the only picture that came to mind was an Iyawo who was dried out—the wood split and cracked. The patterns on this Iyawo's hair were furrows eaten by termites. Sade bent her own head in dismay. She felt herself crumbling.

When Sade next opened her eyes, she was lying on a bed staring at someone misty and fuzzy. Slowly the figure became Miss Harcourt. There was no Mr. Morris, no class, no corridor. She was in a small room full of whiteness. White walls around her, white sheet beneath her, white screen at the end of the bed, white chair beside her. Miss Harcourt asked how she was feeling. Sade barely managed to nod. Everything about her felt heavy, most of all her tongue. She watched the teacher's silky chestnut hair swing lightly as she tilted her head.

"You gave us quite a fright! Passing out like that! Mrs. King is on her way now . . . need a doctor but . . . probably stress. We had no idea . . ."

Sade drifted in and out of listening. It seemed that the school now knew something about Papa. Did that mean they also knew about Mama? Did they know what happened to Mama after the ambulance men carried her away under the blinding white sheet?

She didn't know. She didn't even know if Papa knew. She had not even had a proper chance to ask him.

"If we had known before . . . help . . . cope . . ."

Sade shut her eyes and her ears.

Aunt Gracie's doctor came to the house and declared he could find nothing wrong with her. His eyes twinkled behind thick round glasses, like those of a friendly Brown Owl. Once again Sade heard the word "cope."

"It must have been all too much to cope with, Mrs. King. Even for an adult, you know, it would be too much. What the child needs is rest. And you must encourage her to eat more."

Aunt Gracie led the doctor out of the pineapple-colored bedroom to the door.

"I think she finds it hard to eat because her father has stopped . . ."

The hushed tones trailed down the stairs, out of Sade's hearing.

CHAPTER 37

BLAME

AUNT GRACIE COAXED SADE with a bowl of soup. She brought it into the bedroom on a small tray brightly painted and labeled FLOWERS FROM JAMAICA. Sade avoided looking at her, staring instead at the scarlet imitations of flowers that looked like flaming forest buds.

"My mother made the very same chicken broth, you know. She used to say, 'It build you up, so you better drink up!'"

"But I'm not hungry, Auntie," Sade tried to protest.

Aunt Gracie lifted Sade's hand, smoothing it between her own.

"I know," she said gently. "But your mama would have wanted you to eat."

It was the first time Aunt Gracie had mentioned Mama. Something silently burst, like the air exploding in Sade's ears up in the airplane. It was scary. Like entering somewhere new and strange.

"I'll try, Auntie," she whispered. She forced herself to take sips from the bowl, but was relieved when Aunt Gracie left her and she could block out all thoughts in sleep.

When she woke, the light outside was already fading. Femi must have come back from school, but Aunt Gracie had probably asked him not to disturb her. She pulled the curtains and turned on the desk light. In the yellow glow, her room looked comforting. She reached for her felt pens and a piece of thin white card from a batch she had discovered in the bottom desk drawer. Resting a folded piece of card on the Flowers of Jamaica tray, she sketched a flaming forest tree with sweeping umbrella branches stretching out across the paper. Then an equally tall pawpaw tree next to it, as elegant as a straight-backed woman carrying a jar of water on her head. Underneath, sprouts of lemongrass. She could almost smell the lemongrass from the backyard at home.

For a short while she was totally absorbed in drawing and coloring. Then she opened the card and on the inside printed in curling letters:

To Mariam's Mother and Uncle and Mariam,
Happy Christmas
from Sade

She sat for a while with her pen poised above the opposite page, trying out different words in her head. Finally she simply wrote at the top:

I am very sorry.

The space beneath looked bare and empty. Perhaps she could draw a magnolia like the one outside Papa's study. But when she tried to imagine it closely, her mind went blank. She felt panic. What would Mariam's family think about the card? They were Muslims and wouldn't celebrate Christmas anyway! Would they accept her apology? She might as well tear up the card! She held it open, staring at her message, each hand pulling at the card as tightly as it could. But her hands balanced each other and the paper did not rip. Suddenly she was shaking with rage.

Sade shoved the card and pens into the desk drawer and flung herself back under the quilt. She had only got into this trouble because of Madams Marcia and Donna. If only she had never set eyes on them! She never wanted to be in the same school. Not even the same country. She just wanted to be at HOME. LAGOS NOT LONDON. She hadn't chosen to come. Her head throbbed. Why did Papa have to write all those things that upset the Brass Button Generals? Why didn't he just keep away from people who meant trouble? Like Mariam's uncle said—"Just Keep Away."

The door to her bedroom creaked open. Sade thrust her head above the cover as Femi poked his head around the door with a finger in front of his lips.

"Aunt Gracie said to let you sleep," he confided.

"Get out!" Sade screamed. "GET OUT!"

Startled, Femi ducked away. But Sade had seen the fear in his face.

She buried her face. Whatever had come over her? Whatever was she thinking?

Evil enters like a needle and spreads like an oak tree.

If Mama could see her now, that's what she would say. You are letting evil enter your heart. How can you think of blaming your own father!

Sade trembled as she imagined Mama's eyes and voice. She should make herself face the truth. She had been avoiding it. Mama's eyes were telling her to look into herself. Yes, it really was because of her that Mama had died. She had always been so slow in preparing her schoolbag. Femi had been ready that day. She was the one who had held him up. Kept him waiting. Her nightmares reminded her. That was why they always started with her packing her books. In slow motion. Waiting and waiting to hear Mama's scream. If only they had set off earlier that day, the gunmen would have missed them. Joseph would have shut the gates—and Mama would still be alive.

CHAPTER 38

FACE TO THE WALL

WHEN AUNT GRACIE CAME with fresh orange juice, Sade lay silent with her face to the wall. The orange juice was untouched when Aunt Gracie came again with supper. Sade remained turned away from her. Aunt Gracie gave up, taking the plate of chicken and rice back downstairs.

I deserve to be punished, Sade thought. I don't deserve a friend like Mariam. Or Aunt Gracie and Uncle Roy or Mama Appiah or Iyawo-Jenny or Mr. Nathan or even Miss Harcourt . . . Everyone who had tried to help, one way or another, had actually been deceived. They thought she was worth helping. Even Papa was deceived.

"Sade! News!"

Sade heard Femi's shouts. Tunneling further into the bed, she ignored them and the thumping footsteps up the stairs. Her door flung open.

"We're on TV! With Uncle Dele! I saw the picture—the man said it's after the break! Come, Sade! Please! It's now!" Femi's voice bubbled and pleaded. Even from deep in her burrow, Sade heard a small chink of Femi from the past. The old Femi underneath the skin now fastened as tightly as a drum. Touch the new Femi and he often boomed at you. But she shouldn't have shouted at him earlier. He had suddenly looked so fearful, hurt. It was brave of him to come back into her room. His footsteps squeaked on the landing, then thudded down the stairs.

For a few moments Sade huddled in her cocoon. Whatever was happening to her? She had to drag herself out of the bed. She took herself three-quarters of the way down the stairs and sat down. Peeking through the railings she could see Uncle Dele's head on the television screen at the far end of the sitting room. It was the interview he gave outside the Detention Center.

"My brother is on hunger strike because he is not prepared to be sent away quietly! No one can expect justice in Nigeria as long as the soldiers rule. They hate my brother because he writes the truth! Every week they sent threats. But he refused to give up. Now he has paid a terrible price. His wife has been killed and for weeks his children were lost to him when he sent them to England. The Home Office says it has no record of them—but they are here . . ."

The camera swung to her and Femi. Femi was frowning while she looked so calm!

"My brother came to Britain seeking help. At school we used to hear a lot about the British sense of justice. But we are desperate for deeds as well as words!"

The camera returned to Mr. Seven O'Clock in the studio and another story. Sade did not wait to hear what Aunt Gracie or Uncle Roy had to say. She crept back to her room and crawled into bed. How on earth had she managed to remain so calm in front of the cameras yesterday? She couldn't have done that today. Her feelings frightened her. Like being in one of those little boats she used to watch from Leki Beach. As if far away from land she had been skimming over waves that suddenly turned on her. Whipping and lashing her so wildly that they seized her oars and threatened to sink her.

When the telephone rang, Sade knew it must be Papa. If she pulled her quilt over her head, Aunt Gracie would think she was asleep and leave her alone.

CHAPTER 39

A VISITOR

THERE WERE ONLY TWO more days until the end of term and the doctor had ordered Sade to rest. This time Femi did not argue about staying off school. Sade thought he must be hoping that someone at school had seen him on television. She did not want to think about her school or her class. She did not want to think about anything or anyone.

But when Aunt Gracie came up with juice and a bowl of cornflakes, she brought the news that Mama Appiah was coming to talk to her later in the afternoon.

"Mrs. Appiah says you look so good on television! Like a star! She is sure this will help your daddy."

Aunt Gracie trying to cheer her up made Sade even more miserable. Mama Appiah would as well. She forced herself to eat a few cornflakes so that Aunt Gracie would feel she had at least tried and would take the bowl away. But she still did not feel at all hungry.

Most of the day, Sade lay in bed listening to music on the little radio that Aunt Gracie had put on her desk. She tried reading a book from the school library, but it took too much energy to keep her eyes on the print, even to hold the book.

At least the music filled her brain. Once, however, after she dozed off, she jerked awake, imagining a line of stick-thin people struggling across miles of sand. The figure in front held up his hands in a way that reminded her of someone. The picture came closer, like a television camera moving in, until she was forced to see that it was Papa. At the head of a line of starved refugees. Papa was still talking with his hands.

When the doorbell rang at about four o'clock, Sade rolled over to face the wall again. Perhaps Mama Appiah would not stay if she thought she was disturbing her. Aunt Gracie's voice rang like a warning bell on the stairs.

"It's very good of you to come! Sade will be so pleased to see you! But only for a few minutes. Doctor says she needs plenty of rest. She may even be sleeping now."

Sade waited to hear Mama Appiah's rich tones but there was no reply.

"I have a visitor for you, Sade." Aunt Gracie's words bounced lightly. "Your friend has come to see you."

Sade lay still.

"Your schoolfriend."

Sade lifted herself on to her elbows. Behind Aunt Gracie stood Mariam! She held out a large white envelope.

"We make a card for you. I say I will bring it."

Sade stared at it but did not reach out.

"How very kind of you," said Aunt Gracie. "Isn't that kind of your class, Sade?" Aunt Gracie took the envelope from Mariam and handed it to her. "I shall leave you girls together. But only about ten minutes, mind you!"

Neither girl spoke as Sade slowly lifted the flap and

pulled out a card with a spray of flowers and GET WELL SOON! on the front. A folded piece of notepaper slipped out on to the bed. She left it there while she examined the mosaic of names and messages. Underneath HOPE YOU FEEL BETTER! printed in the center, someone had written AND THAT YOUR DAD IS FREE SOON. She scanned the Good Lucks, Best Wishes and See You Soons. There were names she knew and others for which she did not even know the faces. Strangers to her. But then, tucked away in the bottom left hand corner, she stumbled on *Love, Marcia*. Immediately underneath was *Donna xxx*. The liars! She could feel Mariam waiting for her to say something. Her mouth felt completely dry. Perhaps some of the others also didn't mean what they said.

Don't judge the village by the thief, Sade. If the dog steals, will you punish the goat?

She forced her eyes to circle around the other messages again. Mr. Morris and Miss Harcourt had signed too. Finally her eyes traveled to the message Mariam had been waiting for her to see.

My family wish you get well soon, Mariam.

"Thank you," Sade said softly. "I have got something for you too but I have to finish it." She pulled out the Christmas card and pens from the desk drawer. Mariam sat on the edge of her bed while Sade worked in silence, drawing a row of palm trees in the remaining blank space inside. Swift light-brown strokes made the sand. Underneath, in emerald green, she wrote:

I hope one day you will be able to go home.

She hesitated, wondering whether to add something about Mariam's brother. Maybe it was better not to. Remembering him must be painful for them. Yet it was Mariam who had told Sade about him—even about her father dying in prison. It was something she still had to learn. How to talk about Mama.

She handed Mariam the card, making herself explain that the front was a picture of their backyard at home.

"My brother, Femi, used those trees for his goals."

"My brother, Hassan, also . . . he is crazy about football . . . but now"—Mariam's voice flattened—"now I don't know anything."

Aunt Gracie put her head around the door, reminding them of the time.

"Come whenever you like in the holidays, mi dear. You will be welcome!"

Mariam's grave face opened into a lovely smile. She pointed to the letter on the bed.

"Maybe you like your letter. Morrissy say he is proud someone from his class do what you do."

Sade picked up the piece of folded paper.

"You read, you see. I go now or my mother worry too much." Mariam raised her hand to say good-bye but suddenly halted in midair.

"I nearly forget! Marcia and Donna they in trouble! They have to see headmaster and they not come back to class this afternoon. People say someone father—from Year Seven—come to make big complaint!"

Mariam said good-bye and was gone. Sade briefly

remembered her fantasy of having Papa alongside her to tackle Marcia and Donna. It must have taken courage for that Year Seven child to ignore the threats. But she would rather not think of Marcia and Donna at all—certainly not now. She turned up the radio again and unfolded her letter.

Dear Sade,

All of us in 8M want to send you our warmest wishes and we hope you will have a good rest over the Christmas holidays. Some of the class—and myself— saw you on the Seven O'Clock News on Monday. We have all been shocked to realize what you and your family have been going through. I feel somewhat guilty as I fear you may have thought that you were in some kind of trouble on Monday when I called you out to have a word in private. In fact, it was the very opposite.

After lessons on Friday, I received a telephone call from a producer of the school's program Making News. She told me how you and your brother had very bravely come to tell your father's story to the chief presenter of their channel's news. Apparently he was so impressed by you that he has suggested the topic of refugees for a future Making News. They would like you (and your brother if he would like that) to take part. Class 8M has also been invited to present an investigation for the same program.

Don't worry about deciding now. 8M does not know about the invitation and you should not feel under any pressure. All I have told the class is that you were responsible for getting your father's story reported. He must be very proud of you. We all are and can understand how worried you must still be about him.

I should say that the idea to send you "Get Well" wishes came from members of the class themselves. But they also asked me especially to write that they feel very sad and troubled to hear about your mother's death. We all send much sympathy to you and your brother.

Yours sincerely,
Duncan Morris

CHAPTER 40

WHERE IS PAPA?

CHRISTMAS DREW CLOSER. Mariam's visit and Mr. Morris's letter lifted Sade's spirit a little and she began to spend time downstairs. Christmas cards straddled the mantelpiece and shelves of the bookcase in the sitting room. Tiny painted wooden birds and animals hung between the needles of a small pretend pine tree perched above the television. Aunt Gracie said that the handmade stars and angels sprinkled with glitter had all been made long ago by her children. She was busy with pies, puddings and cakes and invited Sade to help. The grown-up King children were returning late Christmas Eve and there were conversations with friends and neighbors about sofa beds, camp beds and mattresses. But Sade only half listened while she kneaded the cream-colored dough and cut out pastry shapes. This was nothing like any Christmas she knew.

Papa always said they were like homing pigeons. From north, south, east and west, every Solaja and Adewale family made the cross-country journey at Christmas. A map would have shown a magnificent giant spider's web, with dozens of strands drawing in toward Family House. Woven throughout their home village were the houses and compounds of elders like Grandma, Baba Akin, Baba Kayode . . . Christmas meant Grandma, Mama and Papa, uncles and aunts great and small, and endless cousins with their cousins. Christmas meant chasing chickens and goats or climbing "Baba Baobab" (the oldest tree in the world, Femi claimed). Christmas meant listening to Baba Akin's stories (like how he was chased in the forest by iwin when he was a little boy!). First they would watch Baba search the rafters for tobacco leaves, then crush them in his leathery hand and press them neatly with his little finger into his long pipe. Waiting for his pipe to light up was all part of waiting for the story. Christmas also meant cocks crowing in the morning. Waking up ears. Come alive! Come alive! Listen to the sounds of the day! From talking drums in the market to Mama's favorite Christmas carol service on Papa's "This is the BBC World Service broadcasting from London." The little radio always traveled with them.

Christmas Day itself meant the dawn journey to Ibadan. Even Papa came with them to church on this day, making Mama smile with quiet pleasure. Their car hurtled over bumps and potholes in the stony dry track until they reached the main road. Past the hill that Mama climbed every day during the Christmas she had been pregnant with Sade. Mama even called it Sade's Hill.

"I was in training! For a first-class baby!"

They would drive past the palms that fanned out above the bush like gigantic radar wheels in the sky. Past thick tangles of cassava fields. Past the empty grass-roofed roadside stalls.

And finally through the people-filled streets of Ibadan. Up above the thousands upon thousands of rust-red roofs, up to Grandma's church on top of its hill.

Aunt Gracie had mentioned the children's service at her church several times but had not pressed when neither Sade or Femi responded. After the bubble of excitement over Uncle Dele and the TV interview, Femi was once again silent and moody. When Papa rang to speak to them each evening, Femi only mumbled a few words.

Sade could hear their father's voice sounding lighter, weaker. Already over ten days without food! But still he insisted that they should not worry. Letters of support were arriving every day, some with copies of protest letters sent to the Home Office. A university in America even wanted Papa to come and lecture there.

"Listen to this, Sade." Paper rustled at the other end of the line. "'Our students need to hear you. We need more people like you who are prepared to tell those hidden stories. We might not have assassination squads here but there are many other ways of making a journalist keep quiet.'"

Papa was waiting for her to say something. What could she say? *She* needed him. She and Femi needed him. But all these other people said they needed him too. Across another ocean.

"Sade? Are you there?"

"I'm here." Her thoughts darted wildly like the bees smoked out of their hive at the back of Family House.

"Papa, what would Mama think?"

Sade swallowed in awe at her own question. The words had just trickled out of her mouth, thin and clear. She held her breath.

"Probably . . . no . . ." Papa corrected himself softly. "I think she would want me to remember Sade's Hill!"

On the day before Christmas Eve, when the afternoon light was beginning to fade, there were unexpected visitors. Even from the sitting room Sade recognized the voice at the door.

"Shh!" She signaled to Femi to stop jiggling the letters in the Scrabble bag.

"I hope you don't mind us calling round like this! We just wanted to drop off these presents for Sade and Femi. Such poor things! We saw them on telly, didn't we, Kevin? I knew they must've been through something, but I had no idea just how bad! You just don't think, do you?"

They could hear Aunt Gracie's invitation to come inside. There was no way of avoiding the visitors. When Sade and Femi peeped into the hallway, the pushchair with the sleeping twins had already been levered into the hallway.

Mrs. Graham flurried toward them. Caught like a nut in a cracker, Femi stiffened in her hug. But the moment he was released, he escaped upstairs. Kevin stood behind his mother looking awkward. Sade wondered how she could escape too. She knew Mrs. Graham meant well, but her stomach twinged at the thought of answering questions. Aunt Gracie saved her as soon as Mrs. Graham's arms freed her.

"Perhaps you should also go for a rest, Sade."

"Aaah! All this palaver! They're only kids! It's too much

strain for them! You know what I mean?" Mrs. Graham tutted sympathetically to Aunt Gracie. She turned to Sade.

"Before you go, lovie, Kevin has a message for Femi. Right, Kevin?"

Kevin shuffled.

"Tell your brother"—he stumbled, then raised his eyes—"if he wants to play football on Saturdays, he can come with me if he likes. To my club, I mean."

If Kevin had not looked directly at her, Sade would have thought this was his mother's idea. The flicker of nervousness across his face, however, suggested the offer was genuine.

"I'll tell him," said Sade. "But you should ask him yourself."

"Yeah. Another time. I'll call, right?" He bit on his thumb. Just like she did when she was unsure of herself.

"Any friend of Sade or Femi is always welcome," Aunt Gracie offered. The lilt in her voice drew out the word "friend."

When Papa did not call at his usual ten to eight, Sade began to inspect the hallway clock every few minutes. At half-past eight, Uncle Roy rang the prison. Something was wrong.

"Where is he? . . . Why not? . . . I see." Uncle Roy's voice sank. He replaced the receiver slowly.

"Your daddy has been transferred. The man wouldn't say where. We have to ring in the morning to talk to the senior officer."

Uncle Roy and Aunt Gracie exchanged one of those silent eye messages. Just what Mama and Papa used to do when they were worried. The worst thought sneaked into Sade's mind. Before it had time to bury itself secretly, she blurted it out.

"They've taken him to the airport!"

"Hold on, hold on!" Uncle Roy's hands waved as if calming a choir. "Your daddy is probably in hospital," he said slowly. "The man said the doctor has ordered tests."

"Tests?! What kind of tests?"

"I am sure he will be all right." Aunt Gracie's arm slipped around Sade's waist. "Let's talk about it over a cup of tea." Femi moved out of Aunt Gracie's reach but followed them into the kitchen, his eyes sunk deep within his small warrior's mask.

Together they turned over the possibilities. Mr. Nathan's answering machine offered no number for emergencies and the office was closed until after Christmas. Uncle Dele's line was still cut off and Mama Appiah's telephone rang endlessly. There was nothing they could do except wait until the morning.

CHAPTER 41

CHRISTMAS EVE . . . IF

SADE LAY AWAKE, LISTENING for the telephone. Surely Papa would ring if he could. Was he too ill? Or were the hospital tests a cover-up? What better time to get rid of him—while everyone was busy with Christmas. But both Aunt Gracie and Uncle Roy said the government would not risk doing something underhanded while Papa was still in the news.

Of course! Why had she not thought of it before? The news people could find out where Papa was! She jolted up and switched on her desk lamp to search for the paper with the address of the television studio. Mrs. Howe had added the telephone number underneath. She could ring and ask for the newsroom. It was very late, but Papa had sometimes worked on his news all night. With luck, someone would be there.

The landing was dark with no beam of light underneath Aunt Gracie and Uncle Roy's door. Sade crept downstairs by clutching on to the banister. The streetlight glowed eerily through the ruffles of net that veiled the window beside the front door. By shifting the telephone nearer, she could just make out its buttons. As she propped up the paper with the number on the window ledge, the clock in the hallway began to chime. She waited, counting. Twelve. The echo of the final chime covered the pips as she dialed. Holding the mouthpiece close, she asked for the newsroom. Once again she listened to ringing. It kept on ringing. Perhaps no one was there after all. They must have gone home. It was Christmas Eve now. Sade was on the point of giving up when a woman answered, her voice flat and brisk. It seemed to pick up a little interest, however, when Sade said who she was and why she was ringing.

Curled back in bed, in the shadows of her room, doubts began to rise. Even if the reporter found out where Papa was being held, that would not stop him being sent off into the waiting arms of the Brass Buttons and their soldiers. Caught halfway between sleep and wakefulness, Sade could not stop her mind zigzagging. Pictures from the past mingled crazily with thoughts of what might happen. She remembered the night on the airplane, peering out to see their home—and all of Lagos—disappear into a scattering of pinprick lights in the vast darkness. She remembered her feeling then of spinning out into space. Adrift.

How much older she felt now than that Sade of six weeks ago! So much had been frightening, yet somehow she and Femi were still here. Even if her brother kept his misery wrapped up like a hand grenade, at least they were still together. All they needed now was for Papa to be well again and to be allowed to stay with them. Was that too much to ask for? Mama had always said nothing was too much or too little to pray for. But Mama had believed in miracles.

Sade was awakened by Uncle Roy rumbling on to the

landing. Someone was knocking at the front door.

"Who on earth? Seven o'clock—on a Sunday morning!"

Sade threw off her quilt. A sixth sense propelled her out of bed. Aunt Gracie, fastening her dressing gown, joined Sade at the top of the stairs. Femi too came shuffling out of his bedroom in time to see Uncle Roy unbolt the door.

A whirlwind followed. Uncle Roy's deep roar of delight swept upstairs with the open blast of frosty air. Sade and Femi tumbled headlong downstairs. Papa, frail and supported by Uncle Dele's arm, stood smiling in the doorway.

"Take care!" Uncle Dele pitched out his free hand to stop the children bowling Papa over. Swiftly they wriggled as close as possible to their father.

"Lean on me, Papa!" Femi urged.

With Uncle Dele's help they escorted Papa to the sitting room.

After the first flurry of greetings, Papa unraveled his tale. The doctor had become worried about pains in his chest and wanted him to have tests in the hospital. It would be difficult to get them done on a weekend just before Christmas but the doctor had gone away to see what he could arrange. The prison officers, however, seemed more worried that other detainees might riot if anything happened to Papa. They had moved him to another wing of the prison where he was on his own. When he overheard talk about taking him to another prison altogether, he had rung Uncle Dele who in turn rang Mr. Nathan.

"But his office is closed!" Sade interrupted.

"He gave me his home number—for emergencies," explained Uncle Dele.

Mr. Nathan had acted straightaway. Somehow he had managed to speak to a member of Parliament who spoke to the Home Secretary himself. Within hours Papa was taken to a hospital in Oxford and the Home Secretary ordered that he should be set free! Papa could live in England for six months while they decided whether to let the family stay or send them away.

When the hospital said that the tests could only be done after Christmas, Papa had discharged himself.

"I told them that you children would be my best medicine!" Papa stroked their heads. "Your mama always said I was a bad patient. But perhaps she would forgive me this time."

He fell quiet. Sade had never seen their father look so tired. She watched him take small sips of tea. Mama had often reminded him to slow down when he gulped his food in a hurry to get back to his work. Yet today even sipping seemed to take an effort.

Uncle Dele took up the story of how he had brought Papa back from Oxford to London at midnight. They had decided it was too late to disturb the Kings. Sade smiled to herself. She might tell them later about her midnight call to the television newsroom.

"It's my fault we are so early," Papa apologized. "I couldn't wait any longer."

Aunt Gracie laughed and shook her head.

"Good folk get up with the sun," she reassured him. "It's

we who have become lazy! All these clouds in England, you see. They cover up the sun and we forget!"

Papa's brief chuckle touched Sade's memory of Papa of old. Uncle Dele laughed as well, but then turned serious.

"Do you know, Sade and Femi, that you actually saved your Papa?" He gazed earnestly from one to the other. "If you hadn't taken his story to those news people, there could have been a very different ending."

Sade felt herself flush and Femi's lips wavered into a little grin.

"Like for poor Mr. Galib, my teacher friend from Somalia." Papa's face and voice became subdued again. "They sent him back last week. Almost certainly to prison. Such a brave man—" Papa broke off, closing his eyes.

"May God help him," Aunt Gracie murmured, then brought the conversation back to Uncle Dele's tribute.

"Roy and I have been wanting to tell you, Mr. Solaja, that we think you have two special children. They have gone through such a great deal, you know, and they're bearing up!"

"Very true! And it hasn't been easy." Uncle Roy's words rolled out into a silence that caught them all.

Papa was the first to speak.

"There are some things I have been wanting to give you children. I brought them with me"—he paused—"from home."

He signaled to Uncle Dele to pass him a small holdall. He began rummaging down one side, then the other.

"Ah, here they are!"

With a flourish he held up two pairs of red and black

goalkeepers' gloves, one larger than the other. Femi's eyes followed like a cat riveted by butterflies. Papa handed them to him. Femi turned the gloves over to examine them, his eyebrows raised in pleasure.

"Mama bought them for you and me—just before she died," Papa added quietly.

In an instant Femi's face crumpled and distorted in a battle against sobs and tears. He would have dashed from the room, but Papa's arm swooped around him and pulled him onto his lap, pushing aside the bag. Femi buried his head in Papa's chest.

Although Sade felt her own eyes pricking slightly, she somehow knew that this time she was not going to cry. She seemed to have cried so many tears already in the past few weeks. Today it was Femi's turn. She knelt next to Papa, waiting for her brother's sobs to subside. Auntie Grace, Uncle Roy and Uncle Dele slipped quietly out of the room. She and Femi were alone with Papa for the first time since Uncle Tunde had left them together in Papa's study on the day Mama died. That day they were like three survivors clinging to each other, stranded on a tiny raft. Since then they had been flung apart, thrown into so many dangerous rapids. Yet here they were, having finally reached the same shore. Perhaps in a few months they were going to be pushed away again but, for the moment, it was enough that they were together again.

"Look in my bag, Sade."

Papa's arms were still comforting Femi as he directed her to look for a white *agbada*. Her hands delved in to lift it and she felt the weight of something inside. Something solid and heavy. Suddenly she felt light and fluttery, as if the little Christmas tree birds were alive inside her fingers, beating their tiny wings. She unwrapped the material. There, gleaming against the starched white cotton, lay her own ebony Iyawo! Oh, Iyawo was almost alive with her delicately patterned hair and serene, calm eyes! Sade's fingers nimbly unfolded the *agbada*'s matching trousers. It was indeed Oko! Iyawo's own companion with his narrow high-boned cheeks and his eyes still so sorrowful. With Oko cupped between her palms, she stretched to plant a swift kiss on Papa's ear. Then, one at a time, she placed Oko and Iyawo on the mantelpiece between the Christmas cards. A puffy flame-red bird, perched on the shoulder of a snowman, seemed to inspect the newcomers through its beady black eyes.

It was as if Papa knew what she was thinking.

"We're not going to give up hope. Those rogues and thieves in our country won't be there forever. One day we shall go home!" He spoke in that steady voice that Sade had always found so comforting. She nestled back close to Papa and Femi. Home. She still found it so difficult to say the word herself. She would have to learn. Now that Papa was with them, England might become their new "home" for a while, if they were allowed to stay. If Papa was to lecture in America, they might make a new "home" there. If they went to South Africa . . . If, if . . . Wherever they went, they would have to become like tortoises who carry their homes on their backs. She thought of Papa's brave tortoise and hoped that at least they would not have to meet any more leopards.

Sade gazed at Oko and Iyawo and the rich streaks of brown within their glowing ebony faces. She thought of her desk at home and the forest behind Family House from where the wood came. She thought of Grandma. Grandma who had lost a daughter—and whose grandchildren were now thousands of miles away. This Christmas one whole branch of the family would be missing at Family House. Sade suddenly knew what she had to do. Papa and Femi were dozing next to each other and she eased herself away. Cradling Iyawo and Oko in her arms, she made her way carefully upstairs to her desk.

CHAPTER 42

LETTER HOME

24 December,
Christmas Eve

Dear Grandma,

I am very sorry I did not write for a long time. Femi and I couldn't say good-bye to you or anyone. Everything was so horrible. Why are there such wicked people in the world, Grandma? I will never never forget what they did to Mama.

But today Femi and I are happy that Papa is with us again and Uncle Dele is here too. Papa carried my Iyawo and Oko all the way here. They are on the desk in front of me, watching me write. We are staying with Aunt Gracie and Uncle Roy in London. You would like them. They have been looking after Femi and me. Their own children are now grown-up, but they are coming home for Christmas. Just like we always used to visit you, Grandma. If I think about Mama and you and everyone at Family House, I shall start crying again. I didn't know I had so many tears. They would fill up your biggest pot and spill over onto the earth.

Aunt Gracie says that Papa must stay here until Uncle Dele finds somewhere for the four of us. She says that she will fatten Papa so he won't feel the cold so much. She is in the kitchen downstairs cooking the chicken broth that her mama used to make in Jamaica and it smells good.

I miss you very very much, Grandma.

Your loving granddaughter,
Sade

The characters in this story are all fictional. However, we hear about three political figures who were real people. *Ken Saro-Wiwa* was a well-known Nigerian writer. He protested that Ogoniland, his birthplace, had been polluted and robbed by multinational oil companies and the military government. He was hung with eight others in November 1995.

The novel is set immediately after this event, when Nigeria was under the rule of the dictator *General Abacha.* He has since died—quite unexpectedly in 1998—and a year later the government was handed over to a democratically elected president.

The third real figure in the novel is *President Barre,* whom Mariam mentions when telling her story about fleeing from Somalia. Barre was a military ruler who dealt very harshly with rebel groups. In 1988 government planes bombed the city of Hargeisa in northern Somalia. This is where Mariam lived and it was from there that her father was taken by soldiers. The journey, on foot and by donkey, that she made to Mogadishu in the south was over 600 miles. President Barre fled abroad in 1991 and, at the time of writing, Somalia still has no settled central government. The north has been the most peaceful region. It declared itself an independant country—Somaliland—but is still waiting for the world to recognize it.

GLOSSARY

agbada a robe for a man, usually embroidered (Yoruba)

aso-oke a wrap and blouse made from special cloth hand-woven with gold or silver thread (Yoruba)

ayo a wooden board game with sunken "cups," played with pebbles moved at lightning speed (Yoruba)

buba a blouse for a woman (Yoruba)

egungun a traditional Yoruba festival—a masquerade where masked dancers and drummers call on spirits of their ancestors to return to earth to bless them

gari ground cassava, a root vegetable

gele a head scarf for a woman matching her outfit (Yoruba)

harmattan a dry land wind that blows down south from the Sahara for about three months, usually beginning in November

iwin sprites or spirits believed to live in forests (Yoruba)

Iyawo a wife or a bride, partner of *Oko* (Yoruba)

naira Nigerian currency

O dabo! Good-bye! (Yoruba)

Oga, open de door! Master, open the door! (Pidgin English)

Oko husband, partner of Iyawo (Yoruba)

O ma se o! What a pity! (Yoruba)

Open am! Open up! (Pidgin English)

Or we go break dis gate o! Or we shall break the gate! (Pidgin English)

pawpaw a fruit with soft bright-orange flesh and small black seeds (also known as papaya)

peppersoup a soup made with hot chilies

Pidgin English a form of colloquial English that arose between English-speaking traders and speakers of various West African languages. Nigerian Pidgin has its own vocabulary and forms that are particular to Nigeria.

plantain a vegetable like a giant banana

Queen's English Standard English, the official language of Nigeria

Wetin you carry for back? What are you carrying at the back? (Pidgin English)

yam a root vegetable

You think sey I dey play? Do you think I am playing? (Pidgin English)

Yoruba the language of the second-largest group in Nigeria, a vast country in which over 200 languages are spoken